SUMMER
of
MADNESS

Marion Crook

ORCA BOOK PUBLISHERS

Canadian Cataloguing in Publication Data
Crook, Marion, 1941 –
    Summer of madness

    ISBN 1-55143-041-X

    I. Title.
PS8555.R6116S8 1995   jC813'.54   C95-910442-9
PZ7.C76Su 1995

Publication assistance provided by The Canada Council

Cover design by Christine Toller
Cover photographs by Murphy Shewchuk (background);
    Old Masters Portrait Studio (foreground)

Printed and bound in Canada

Orca Book Publishers
PO Box 5626, Station B
Victoria, BC Canada
V8R 6S4

Orca Book Publishers
PO Box 468
Custer, WA USA
98240-0468

10   9   8   7   6   5   4   3   2   1

To the Soda Creek 4-H Club

Chapter 1

"Put it in a lower gear." Kevin looked at the potholes on the road ahead of us as if they were bottomless pits.

"Just hold on or you'll end up under a wheel." I'd been driving this tractor since I was twelve, so I knew it wouldn't go into a lower gear at this speed. I could see the potholes — they were sprinkled over the road like traps — but I wasn't going to reduce speed. I held the steering wheel with one hand for a moment, while I brushed the hair away from my eyes with the other.

"Use both hands!" Kevin's knuckles whitened as he gripped the fender. He braced his feet against the bottom of the tractor seat and leaned away from me. We lurched over the potholes and onto smoother ground as he tried to stay securely on the bouncing, jolting metal.

I felt his irritation like a prickling on my skin. He was upset about something.

"What did your dad say about the calf?" he demanded. Kevin's six inches taller than I am, and since the fender was higher than the tractor seat, he had to lean down and shout to be heard above the noise of the engine.

"I didn't take the message. As she was leaving for the airport Mom told me to get over to the far meadow and pick up a calf that was sick." I guided the tractor through the wood lot, trying to avoid the branches of overhanging trees, and the worst holes in the dirt road.

"It better not be one of those twelve-hundred-pound Charolais or we're in trouble."

I braked slightly and pulled to the left to miss a log

lying half on the road. Kevin's body jerked as the tractor swerved, but he stayed with me. "She wouldn't have sent me after one that big."

At any other time I would have enjoyed the breeze sifting through the poplar leaves and the sunshine angling through the evergreens, dappling light and shadow on the grass below, but I was driving this John Deere tractor far too fast to do anything but concentrate on keeping it on the road and upright. I talked to Kevin without looking at him.

"Dad called Mom on the cellular. One of the men saw the calf when he drove out to the hay field. She wants me to take it back to the barn on the bucket of the tractor, so it can't be one of the big ones. The vet will meet us at the barn."

"Slow down," Kevin yelled at me. I definitely was making him nervous.

"Duck," I yelled back when I saw I was going to cut close to the tree branches ahead. Kevin ducked and a fir bough brushed the top of his head.

He said something sharp, explicit and obscene. "Slow down, Karen!"

I kept the same speed. The road was level. We were in no immediate danger of rolling into death and destruction. He just wanted to be the one driving. "Hang on."

I couldn't hear him grind his teeth or see the expression on his face because I was looking at the road ahead, but I could feel his annoyance spilling over me like the heat from a fire.

"Why did you come over today, anyway?"

"I need to talk to you."

"Yeah?" I took the last curve in the road before the meadow and slowed the tractor. "Can you see it?"

"There!" Kevin's yell in my ear startled me into slamming my foot on the brake. Kevin almost pitched over the tire at the sudden stop. He glared at me. I shrugged.

"Where?" I looked at the field in front of us. The calf

was more important right now than Kevin.

"Karen, you are getting to me."

"The calf," I said.

He turned toward the meadow. "Over there. See? The cow is on the other side of the fence."

I saw the cow, a Hereford. The calf was hard to spot with only the dark brown patch of its side visible in the long grass. Kevin jumped down, walked toward it, then motioned me to bring the tractor closer.

Kevin and I had worked together for many years. When we were little, our mothers visited each other because we lived on neighbouring ranches, and they thought we needed to "socialize." When we were older, we built forts in the woods between our ranches, hideouts in the hay barn and rafts on the lake. Kevin's older brother, Bob, occasionally brought Kevin and sometimes other kids to play, but often it was just Kevin and me. We ran in the woods and played almost everywhere but in the bull pasture and the abandoned quarry. We had been warned away from both those places and left them alone until we were teenagers. Later, we worked on homework and 4-H projects and helped out on each other's ranches. When I was in the seventh grade and Kevin was in the eighth, he decided that boys were somehow contaminated by girls, and they certainly didn't have girls as best friends. So he ignored me at school, but he still came over to talk and work on projects at home. Kevin had a dual personality that year, but somehow got himself together into one person, and by my eighth grade, he was back to being my best friend.

We had been such friends that we had been able to feel each other's sadness and anger, fears and joy, even when we were apart. I couldn't actually see into his mind, but I used to know, with certainty, what he was feeling. It would come to me like a smell or a touch. It seemed natural then; it seemed weird now that I was sixteen, almost seventeen, and he was almost eighteen. I knew that most people don't connect this way. It was more than sympathizing with each other; it was *feeling* each other, and I didn't like it. Kevin was not my idea of heartthrob city, and I didn't want any special mind-to-mind connection with him now. We had been friends, but I didn't know how long we would stay friends, because he'd been acting moody and angry the last few months.

I inched the tractor closer until he yelled, "Hold it!"

The clutch had a lot of back pressure, and I clenched my hands around the wheel with the effort it took to hold it down. I reached for the controls and slowly lowered the bucket.

"That's it!" Kevin held up his hand. I put the tractor in neutral, flipped the lever down to hold the brakes and jumped to the ground.

The calf, a brown, warm bundle of life, was unconscious, but breathing. Spittle drooled from its mouth; the muscles of its legs twitched. As I watched, its back arched and its whole body shuddered.

"This is bad." Kevin's voice was soft with concern. He knelt at its head and slid his hands underneath it. The calf probably weighed two hundred pounds. I slipped my hands under its hind quarters and we heaved, shoved and rolled it into the bucket.

"It's going to flip right off this." I stared at the convulsing body.

"I'll ride up here with it," Kevin said. "Take it easy on the road."

I hurried to the back of the tractor, climbed on and headed for the barn. I drove more slowly on the drive back, but still too fast for the road. It's a good thing Kevin is strong, because a weak man would have flown out of the bucket when I hit the potholes. The calf's mother followed us, but couldn't keep up with the tractor. I hoped this calf wouldn't die. It was funny. We tried so hard to keep the animals alive and healthy, and then we sold many of them for meat. I'd never quite figured out why we cared so much and worked so hard only to have them die in the end.

We rounded the corner of the barn just as the vet's truck pulled in with our two Border collies yapping and barking around its wheels. The dogs were expert herders and so well trained they won prizes at the cattle competitions, but you wouldn't know it watching them go crazy when anyone drove into our yard. I drove past Kevin's truck and into the corral, stopped the tractor, let the bucket down and shut off the motor. I glanced behind me.

"You still there, Kev?"

"No thanks to your driving." I ignored that. He'd been criticizing my driving for years.

"Is it still alive?" I moved around the tractor and stared at the calf. I felt a sense of frustration, even a hint of anger, coming from Kevin, as if I'd walked into a dense wall. I ignored it. I didn't want to deal with anyone's feelings right then, not even my own.

"Yeah, but it's having seizures." I could see that. Shudders seemed to be rippling through it, jerking muscles and pulling it around wildly as if life was finished with it and giving it a last shake before leaving a carcass.

The calf's mother burst through the trees at a lumbering half-canter, bellowing her fear. She stopped at the edge of the woods.

The vet stood beside the calf, staring at it for a second, and then walked back to her truck.

"What can you tell me about this one, Karen?" I stood beside her while she threw up the panel on the equipment box. I watched her take out a bottle of medicine and fill a syringe. Reena is about five foot seven, not as tall as I am, and she is thinner, with blond hair shorter than Kevin's and the biggest, bluest eyes I've ever seen.

"Not much. Dad just called to let us know it needed help before he called you. What did he say?"

"Not much. 'Emergency. Calf down. Unconscious.' One of the men had reported it. Your dad hadn't seen it."

She turned back to the calf. "I'll give it my best guess then. Shouldn't be hard, since I've seen a lot of this lately." She studied the calf again, listened to its heart with her stethoscope and then injected the medicine. Kevin and I watched the calf. Reena crouched down beside us. "Oh, good," she said.

I let my eyes travel over the calf, but didn't see anything that was good. "What's happening?"

"It's coming out of it." Reena put her stethoscope on the calf again and listened.

"How can you tell?" But, even as I asked, I could see the calm that settled over it like an invisible blanket, the slower, more normal rise and fall of its ribs, and the flicker of its eyelids as it regained consciousness. I changed my question. "What was in that bottle?"

"Atropine. I thought this little guy might have organophosphate poisoning. And I guess he did." The calf shook its head and started to struggle. We stepped back, giving it room. It staggered a little, slowly moving its head from side to side like a newborn, then stuck out its jaw and gave a surprisingly strong cry for its mother.

She answered and ran a little closer, her bag swinging against her legs. We moved away so she could see her baby.

"Ah, another miracle," Reena said. "From unconscious to okay in seconds, and for that I only charge a modest fee. Most miracle workers would want half your ranch, but not me. I'm not greedy. I'm generous, altruistic and a phenomenal vet. Today, I am charging extra, though. You have to give me coffee and food or I may not survive to make my next call."

I blinked, a little slow to respond. Reena takes some

getting used to. She moved here only about six months ago, but already she is the vet most ranchers call. She is smart, efficient and fast, and not only is she a good vet, she grew up on a farm, so she knows a lot about what is important to ranchers.

"Sure," I said. "Mom left dinner cooking in the oven. Kevin, put the tractor in the shed, okay?"

"What about the cow and calf?" He swung up onto the tractor.

"They'll be all right, I guess?" I looked at Reena for advice.

"Leave Mamma where she is on the outside of the pen and the calf in here. I'll shoot it up with atropine again before I leave. If a calf responds to atropine the first time, it's usually fine."

I picked up on what she had not said. "Sometimes they don't respond?"

"That's right. Sometimes they die. Kaput! Very nasty. You're going to have to look over the ranch for that organophosphate or another calf might end up the same way. It's probably fenthion, *Wipe Out*, a dewormer. Usually applied along the ridge of the back and the top of the tail. It's in a bottle and sometimes a spray can. Have to use gloves with it. Nasty stuff. People don't use it much anymore because it's so dangerous." She handed me the bottle of atropine. "Keep this handy. You might need it."

I put the bottle in my pocket and walked beside her. "Would you have time to report to Dad? He's got a haying crew in the north meadow."

She glanced at me out of the corner of her eye and smiled. "Nope. I don't have time. You phone him while I eat."

Reena followed me to the house and up the stairs to the porch. We stopped and looked over a small grass patch to the lake. Today, there was a slight breeze lapping the blue water into waves. Reena took a deep breath. "Gorgeous," she said.

It was. Our ranch starts at the end of Misty Lake and spreads into the ranching district to the north. My friend Paula's ranch sits at the south end, and Kevin's ranch lies along the west shore. There are a few cabins on the east side and a public beach in the government property near Kevin's place. The road through the government timber to the lake is so rough that few people drag their boats through it, so the lake, even in the summer, is almost private for the three ranching families.

A Steller's jay hopped onto the rail of the porch, cocked its tufted head, flashed its blue wings, then called loud, harsh chatter at us as it flew off.

"Cheeky soul," Reena said. "He almost seems to be trying to tell us some gossip."

We left our shoes on the closed-in porch where everyone left everything. Pails were stacked by the window, a new bag of chicken feed was waiting to be carried out to the hen-house. I suppose our house looked messy to most people.

The kitchen smelled of savoury stew, almost as if Mom were still home.

"Take a plate off the top of the pile." I gestured to the counter. "Oh, the bathroom is right there." I pointed toward a back door. "Meat's in the oven, rolls are in the warming oven and everything else is in the fridge or on the table. I'll call Dad."

"You spoil me," Reena said as she headed for the bathroom while I dialled Dad's cellular number. "I had no idea how much I'd enjoy pampering until I moved to Ashton. Years of elegant restaurants, soft music and glittering chandeliers didn't prepare me for the fabulous, hospitable, sophisticated meals of the Cariboo." Her voice disappeared into the sound of water running.

I heard the whine of machinery as Dad answered his phone. "Hey, Karen. Did Mom get away all right?"

"I guess so. She's not here."

"Okay. What about the calf?"

I told him what Reena had said. He understood the importance of the poison. "We'll look for it, but it may be too dark today before we have time." He was silent for a moment. "It doesn't make sense anyway. We haven't had any of that around for years."

I couldn't remember ever seeing it. "Reena says it's deadly."

"I know. How's the calf?"

I could imagine Dad sitting on the forklift, trying to concentrate on picking up the huge round bales and listening to me at the same time. Right now, he didn't need details. "Fine."

"A crew is coming in for dinner in about ten minutes. The next shift will be in about nine."

"Okay." I looked at the table, always set for a meal, and checked that there were at least twenty knives and forks in the centre island container, napkins, ketchup and salt and pepper.

I hung up as Reena passed me on her way to the table with a plate full of beef stew, whole wheat rolls, salad and a glass of milk. She started to eat.

I grabbed a headband from the kitchen junk drawer and bound my hair back. Then I looked over the meal preparations.

Glasses. I checked the side counter. Plenty of glasses. I flipped open the dishwasher. Empty. Mom must have really worked to get everything done before she left. The light on the coffee urn was red, which meant it was ready. The sugar was on the table. Cream. I opened the fridge and set the cream pitcher beside the big fifty-cup coffee urn, then picked up a plate and filled it with stew for myself. Reena's phone rang as Kevin came in the back door. She let it ring three times while she finished her last bite of stew, then pulled it out of her bag, answered and listened.

"On my way," she said. "First turn past the Stewartson Ranch and then five miles north? Fine. No, just keep it inside and away from water until I get there. No, that's okay. I just ate."

Kevin drowned his stew with ketchup and shot Reena a mock serious look. "Everyone knows they have to feed you or you won't come."

"A woman needs standards," Reena said as she stood. She reached into a side pocket of her vest for her invoice book and wrote the bill to us so fast that the pen seemed to have energy of its own.

"The last vet you guys employed died of starvation. I bet you didn't know that. He just kept answering calls until his body shrivelled from lack of food. Struggling, dedicated, he answered call after call without a thought to how he was going to keep his strength up." She tore the bill off the pad and handed it to me. "His colleagues tried to tell him that the ranchers in this area would use him and abuse him until there wasn't a drop of blood left in his body, but would he listen? No, he kept on being devoted and. . . . "

"Dedicated," Kevin suggested.

"Well, there you have it," Reena said as she slung her outsized purse over her shoulder. "You wouldn't want that to happen to me."

"Absolutely not, Reena," I said as I walked to the door with her. "You're just too fantastic to lose."

She patted my cheek. "Only a truly intelligent woman like you would appreciate me." She smiled. "Are you showing in the 4-H sale on Saturday?"

"My sister is showing in the feeding ewe class. I've got a demonstration to do. Are you judging?"

"No. I'd make too many enemies that way. But I'll be there. See you then. Bye, Kevin."

Kevin waved at her from his seat at the table. "See you."

I stopped on my way back to the table and checked on

the amount of coffee in the urn.

"You'd better finish your dinner or you might not get any tonight." Kevin indicated my cooling plate. He was right.

"Are you going to the 4-H show?" he asked me as I ate.

"Mmmm," I said around a mouthful of stew. I swallowed. "Sarah's got some entries, so I have to be with her. Mom's away for three weeks, you know."

"Yeah. What I was really thinking about was the dance."

I looked up. "We usually go to the dance, Dad and Sarah and Mom and me. We'll probably go on Saturday, even without Mom."

He took a deep breath, glanced away and then back at me. "Don't be so dense, Karen. You know I want you to go with me."

I snapped at him. "No, I didn't know you wanted me to go with you." Was I supposed to read his mind? I stared at him. I knew he was frustrated without knowing why. I didn't understand what his problem was. Ever since he'd grown six inches last summer, and developed all those muscles in his shoulders and back, he'd started being moody and tense and irritated with me. Mom said he was having trouble with his hormones, but I didn't see why *I* should be upset by them. I had hormones too. I didn't go around making everyone else miserable.

"Why don't I just meet you there? I've got a whole lot of stuff to do. . . . " I froze when his hand shot out and held my chin. I stopped talking.

"You're not listening to me, Karen." My skin under his hand tingled. I wondered if he would feel the same thing if I touched his chin. I stared at it. He'd been shaving for years, but I'd never really looked at his chin before. It was rougher than mine, and dark, with a shaded beard. I glanced at his eyes. They were big, brown and, at the moment, flashing with irritation.

I shook my head free and sat back. "Okay. I'm listening."

He folded his arms on the table and leaned forward. "I want to pick you up. I want to take you on a date and I want to kiss you when I bring you home."

I blinked. "Uh, Kevin. This isn't on my agenda."

"I know." He looked more exasperated than loving.

We heard the trucks pulling into the yard right then. I stood, reached for his empty plate and moved toward the dishwasher. He shook his head and followed me. The men were at the back door now.

"Wake up, Karen. There's a real world out there," he whispered.

I stared at him.

"Think about the dance."

I grabbed his arm as he turned away. "Not before Saturday. I haven't got time to think of anything before Saturday. I'll see you there." I wasn't used to thinking before I spoke with Kevin, and I just blurted out what I wanted.

He whirled so that his back was to the door. "Don't go with anyone else."

"Okay. Okay." I raised my hands in exasperation. He turned and nodded at the men coming in.

I reached for the oven door, opened it and pulled the stew out so it was easier for the crew to dip into it, then put the salad on the table. I didn't see Kevin leave.

The men were gone in fifteen minutes. We were all working fast and hard right now, with acres of hay to get in before the rain came. Dad said we had three thousand round bales under cover and five hundred more to get. At about a ton a bale, we should have enough to feed the cattle for the winter — if a drizzling August rain didn't ruin the last of the hay. The crew had stacked their dishes in the dishwasher so all I needed to do was turn it on, but they had eaten almost all the rolls and the salad bowl was empty. I found two dozen rolls in the freezer and put them in the warming oven. They should be toasty by nine.

The salad took more time.

While I was rinsing, chopping and mixing, I thought about Kevin — a waste of time. He wasn't making any sense these days. Kiss me? I didn't want him to kiss me and ruin a perfectly good friendship. He'd kissed me before when we were twelve. We'd been watching TV, some kind of soap opera, and we decided to try kissing the way they did on the screen. He put his mouth on mine and I kissed him back. It was like kissing my calf. We hadn't tried it since and I hadn't even *thought* about trying it with him. He was my friend, not my boyfriend.

Now Trevor Foster in my class was someone I seriously thought about kissing. He was tall, with curly hair, dark eyes and an intensity that let me know he really saw me. He'd only been at our school for a year and I didn't know him very well, but I wanted to.

I'd run into him outside the gym one afternoon when I was heading into my karate class. I had been looking down trying to make sure that my *gi* was tied. He backed away from his locker and we collided. He reached out a hand to steady me and I looked up. Dark eyes; all I could see were dark eyes.

"You okay?" he asked.

I stared at him. "Uh, yeah." His hand was still on my arm, a big hand. I suddenly felt small and fragile.

"Hey, you must be tough," he said, dropping his hand. "You're taking karate."

"I'm only a beginner."

"Don't let her hit you, Trevor," Mike called from somewhere behind me. "These ranch girls are strong."

"Would you hit me?" He raised his eyebrows.

I shook my head and said seriously, "No."

He smiled.

"Maybe we could go out sometime?"

"Uh, maybe," I said, and ran to class.

I still go hot all over when I think of how awkward I was. Why hadn't I said something smart like, "Sure. Call me" or "When?" or something provocative and exciting instead of "Uh, maybe," like some starry-eyed, dumb, grade-school kid. Had he meant that he really wanted to go out with me, or had he just been teasing, making fun of me? I never know what to say to guys at school. I don't know what they're thinking or feeling. I don't even know what *I'm* feeling.

It seems that everyone but me knows how to talk and flirt and exchange feelings. I'm competent at some things: math, science, even organic chemistry. I can look after the house, my sister and my animals, but if they gave grades for understanding emotions, I'd get an "F." I can't figure out the simplest relationship. My friend Paula says there is nothing simple about relationships, but *she* seems to understand them.

My mind drifted back to Kevin. Maybe a relationship with Kevin would be exciting. I could ask Mary-Jo Renton; she dated him most of last year. On the other hand, Kevin would probably be a disaster. I hadn't any idea how to have a relationship and I didn't have time. I had real problems to deal with, concrete problems that Mom had left for me. I was going to have three weeks crammed full of work. That was the "real world" I had to deal with. Feelings could wait.

I concentrated on my conversation with Mom this afternoon.

"Be sure to get the meals ready on time," she had said. "I know you can. It's just harder than you think at first."

"Sure, Mom." She'd left pages of instructions in a notebook. Several pages were labelled "Sarah." My little sister had a schedule that would make an air-traffic controller look lazy.

"Grandma isn't going to be sick for a month, is she?"

Maybe this operation was more serious than I knew.

"Not sick. Just helpless. Her hip surgery went fine. She'll be home tomorrow, but she won't be able to do much for herself for about three weeks or more. I promise you I'll be back in three weeks if I have to hire someone to come and look after her, but I couldn't stand to have her come home without me in the house. Someone has to be there."

"It's okay, Mom. Really." She had to go; I had to stay. End of discussion. I glanced at the list again and tried not to look as worried as I felt.

Mom knew, though. "Just call me if you have any questions, or ask Dad. Sarah pretty well knows her own schedule, but she's only ten years old and. . . . "

"It's okay, Mom." I really saw her right then, her smooth forehead crinkling with anxiety, her bright eyes checking the counters as if reassuring herself that the house was safe and wouldn't disintegrate when she left. She's so different from me: short where I'm tall, size eight where I'm size twelve, and short, thick, curly hair instead of the long, thin, straight, fine hair I inherited from Dad's side of the family. She understood people too, where I didn't. Some feelings were obvious, though. She was worried, and she didn't need to worry more than she already was about me, Dad, Sarah and the rest of the world. "We'll be fine. That's a great suit. You look good."

She pushed her curly hair away from her face and stuffed her wallet into her shoulder bag. "Thanks. Okay. I'm going. The plane leaves at six. I have to be there a half-hour ahead of time. Dad will see that the car gets back here." She then rattled off more instructions. "Pick up Sarah from Mary Jane's place when you drop the mail off in the morning. Don't let her watch violent movies and see that she feeds her sheep. Don't let her go near the old quarry. There's a straight drop onto the rocks below." I knew all about the old quarry. Kevin and I used to play there when we were a little older than Sarah just *because* it was dangerous. "I'm sorry you can't get to the lake with Susan for the girls' night out, but. . . . "

"Mom, just go."

She grinned and hugged me fiercely for a moment. Then the phone rang. It was Dad calling about the calf, and Mom sent me off to rescue it.

Mom was so worried about Grandma. I guess I'd feel the same if Mom was the one with the broken hip. I'd want to be with her. I understood Mom had to go, but Edmonton is a long way from us, and I had to do her job — all her jobs: feeding the crews and the animals, delivering the mail, delivering Sarah and picking her up from her friends' houses, running Sarah around to her appointments and answering the phone. My mom ran her life in fifteen-minute segments, like a high-powered executive, and I wasn't sure I was ready for her schedule. My neck muscles hurt just thinking about it. But worry wasn't going to help. In three weeks I'd be back at school, Sarah would be back at school, Kevin would be away at college, the haying should be finished and the 4-H sale and exhibition would be over. I just had to make it through the next three weeks without a major disaster.

Dad brought the crew in at nine. "The stew smells wonderful."

He sounded tired. I smiled at him. He hugged me. "Only one person to hug tonight? Where's Sarah?"

I slid my eyes around the table checking that nothing was missing. "At Heather's place for the night."

"Oh. Seems kind of quiet without her." The men were talking, someone had turned the TV on for the news, the swather, its blades spinning slowly, now chugged into the yard, adding a bass boom to all the noise in the house, but Dad was right. It wasn't the same without Sarah's high voice.

"Are you going to give us a song tonight, Dan?" one of the men called.

Dad shook his head. "I'm not in the mood for the pipes right now, Lyle. Not just now." Dad only played his bagpipes to please himself.

"So, Karen," Mike Larson, a guy from Kevin's class at school called to me from his place at the table. "What was wrong with the calf?" Mike and I had had biology together last year; we both want to be vets. I knew he was as interested in the nature of the problem as he was concerned about the calf.

"*Wipe Out*," I said. "Poison."

There was a sudden silence. All the men turned to me.

"My brother lost two last week," one of the men said slowly. "Twitching and convulsions, he told me."

"We've lost two in two weeks," Mike offered. "Same sort of seizure-type stuff. My dad thought maybe it was some kind of poisoned weed."

No one spoke for a moment. Dad looked over at Lyle Jennings, my friend Paula's father. "How many at your place?"

"One," Lyle said.

"There was one this week at Kevin's place," I offered.

There wasn't a sound from the men at the table. The TV gave the weather report into the silence.

Here it comes, I thought. A major disaster.

Chapter 2

My alarm dragged me out of sleep the next morning at six. I was glad of the steam from my shower that produced a blurred image in the clouded mirror. I didn't really need to see myself in all-revealing detail. My eyes were dark smudges in a pale face, the freckles invisible. My hair blended into the shower curtain behind me, my body into the dark towel I held. I looked like a floating face, a ghost, something on late-night TV that flickers across the screen and then disappears into darkness. The truth was, I felt like a ghost, a little unearthly and separated from my body by sleep deprivation.

I had managed to pour myself a cup of coffee and was sitting at the kitchen table by 6:30. The house was quiet. Dad had already gone to the fields, leaving me a note beside the coffee urn: "Lunch at one, supper at six. We should be finished haying today." Good. I didn't want to do all that cooking for too many days in a row. I had my own work to do.

In the barn, Edie, my calf, sniffed my hand as I checked her water and measured her feed.

"I know, it's early. There should be some law against getting out of bed before nine." I scratched her head. She butted my hand out of her way, stretched her neck and licked my face. I laughed and hugged her. Edie was affectionate and my favourite calf. She was a heifer, EC-17 on her ear tag, and my current 4-H project. The work I did in 4-H eventually made money for me, since all my calf projects were part of my own herd. By the time I graduate from high school, I should have eight cows in my herd producing a calf crop for me every year. When I leave home for college, Mom and Dad will look after them. While I live at home, I do the work.

I fed Edie, then took the pitchfork and cleaned the worst messes out of the stall, but I left the "two-hour-down-to-the-boards-and-get-it-right" job for another day.

A small pen outside the barn held Sarah's sheep. Since Sarah had spent the night with her friend Heather and wouldn't be back until I picked her up this morning, I had her chores to do as well as my own. Pansy, Sarah's ewe lamb, was so tame she was a nuisance. She wanted food and bleated her complaints the minute she saw me. Typical. Pansy was never satisfied. She was self-centred, whiny and demanding.

"Hold on, Pansy," I tried to calm her. "I'm moving as fast as I can."

As soon as the barley, oats and corn mixture hit the trough, Pansy's head was down; she ate as if Sarah hadn't fed her in months. I gave her fresh water, then walked back to the house.

Supper for the hay crew was next. I studied Mom's instructions and recipes in the notebook, threw together all the ingredients for chili and left it simmering in the oven. By nine, I had finished in the kitchen and was on my way to the mail drop at the highway. Among other things, Mom is the mail lady.

I rolled down the windows and cranked up the stereo. My truck is my joy. It's ten years old, with a few dents in the side where a bull headed it one spring and patches of rust on the bottom where the salt from the winter roads ate the paint, but it runs well, and it's mine. Dad gave me the keys on my sixteenth birthday and told me that since I'd been driving it for two years on the ranch and hadn't hit anything worth mentioning, I could drive it on the road.

He taught me how to change the tires and the wind-shield wipers and how to check the radiator and the transmission fluid. When anything went wrong with it, he had a spare part around that he installed. To make it really feel like mine, I had bought a stereo and speaker system at the secondhand store and Kevin had helped me wire them in. Now rock music started when the engine turned over, blasting loud and wild as I drove. I let the beat bang back and forth in my head, taking the strain of the morning away with it until, by the time I pulled into the rest stop at the highway, I was smiling.

When I turned off the motor, the silence settled on me like dust. There was no traffic on the highway, no airplanes overhead, no tractors in the field and no animal cries — just the still morning air. A flicker flew erratically over the ditch and into the stubble of the fields in front of me, flashing its cinnamon wings. There was no place for it to hide there. The grass had been mowed and the hay hauled away to storage last weekend. The field belonged to Kevin's family.

I suddenly thought that Kevin hadn't told me why he wanted to see me yesterday. He'd been upset about something. The dance? No, but *something* had been bothering him. Maybe I'd ask him about it on Saturday, and maybe I'd just pretend I hadn't noticed.

I unlocked the postbox, pulled out the bag of letters and dumped them on the seat of my truck. Mom's note-book listed the last names of the people on the twenty-mile circle in order of delivery. I knew everyone, but it helped to have them listed as I sorted through the mail and put elastics around the individual deliveries. When I had all the mail separated, I headed out, music blasting rhythm and wailing combinations of sound and gravel spitting staccato notes on the underside of my truck.

I delivered five batches of mail before I pulled into the

Black Creek Reserve, snapping the stereo off as I passed under the yellow log archway that marked the entrance. They have a noise bylaw on this part of the Sushwap Nation land; I didn't need to be picked up by the special constables. The road looped in a large circle around the village, with homes on the outside of the circle and a big field in the centre. Swings and a teeter-totter stood like Tinkertoys at one side of the field, and a baseball diamond with bleachers at the other. No one was playing anywhere on the field; it was too hot. Dust swirled up off the first base line as I drove past. I pulled into Alphonse and Mary Jane Charley's driveway, grabbed their mail and walked to the back of the house.

My sister, Sarah, burst out the door. "Go away!" she yelled at me. She was an exploding bundle of firecracker energy, as usual. "You can't come so soon. We haven't finished our record books yet, and we need them for Friday and the 4-H show, and we haven't finished our display yet, and you're early!" Her straight dark hair bounced into her eyes and she pushed it away impatiently. "So go away, okay?"

She stood in my way, daring me to move past her. Sarah is tall for her age, sturdy, but quick on her feet. She is also opinionated, self-confident and pugnacious.

I took a deep breath and heard my Mom's voice in my head. Listen. When kids talk to you, listen. "So, what's the problem, Sarah?"

Heather's mother, Mary Jane, had followed Sarah to the doorway and stood there, the sun burnishing her dark hair with a mahogany sheen. I know how busy she is, yet she waited as if this moment was more important than anything else in her day.

Sarah slowed her delivery a little. "It's like this, Karen. Heather and me have a lot to do before tomorrow, and we aren't finished."

I smiled at Mary Jane. Sarah's friend, Heather, slipped

out the door to stand beside her mother. She is the oldest child of Mary Jane and Alphonse and has Mary Jane's eyes and chin, but she doesn't have her mother's beautiful hair. Hers is plain brown, like mine. She is the same height as Sarah, but heavier, and is Sarah's opposite in temperament — reasonable where Sarah is emotional, organized where Sarah is impulsive and a little dull where Sarah is fun.

Heather and I are typical oldest children: determined, responsible, hardworking, focused and a little boring. My home-ec teacher told my class at school that birth order determined personality. It bothered me then and it does now to think that I act as I do because I am the oldest child. Predictable. Reasonable. Responsible. Boring. Don't we have any choice? Couldn't we be artistic, impulsive, sexy and exciting? Are we *fated* to be responsible?

"They're not finished, Karen." Mary Jane shook her head. "Such perfectionists."

"So I hear." It was probably Heather who was the perfectionist. Sarah always planned to do more than was possible and didn't finish what she started. "I don't have time to come back. Sorry, Sarah."

Sarah was a lot of trouble. She and Heather almost lived together, either at Heather's place or at ours. Mom and Mary Jane spent a lot of time driving them back and forth.

"You're not helping, Karen. Come on!" Sarah pulled at my shirt. She thinks that if she just talks long enough and loud enough the world will turn the way she spins it.

I looked at Mary Jane. "I really can't come back. We're haying and Mom's away and. . . . "

"Uh-huh. And I can't bring her over later. I have to be at work at one." Mary Jane has three kids and a half-time job at the grocery store, so she doesn't have much time to taxi Sarah around.

I handed Mary Jane her mail. "Could Heather come to our place? The problem is, I'm going to be really busy and. . . . "

"And they could burn the place down before you noticed?"

"Something like that." I waited for Mary Jane to speak or for an idea to come to me.

"I'm ten years old! I'm not a baby." Sarah was indignant.

Don't take away her dignity. My mom was speaking in my ear again. I squatted down to Sarah's level. "We didn't really mean that you would do something that stupid, Sarah. Not really. It's just that you must have a sitter, you know that. It's not optional. Mom would kill me if I left you and Heather alone. Dad would have a fit. Alphonse would sue. I can't take Heather home and not be responsible for her. It just won't happen, kid."

"I'll be responsible for Heather." Sarah thought she could do anything. She would try almost anything because she was so sure of herself. So far she's had a broken wrist and a concussion, but Mom says she has a great spirit. It's hard to let her have her "spirit" and keep her safe.

Mary Jane offered a solution. I suppose three kids made her an expert at juggling schedules. "Could you pick up Heather here at this time tomorrow so she can go with you on the mail route and spend the day at your house? Could you handle them tomorrow?"

"Yeah. Tomorrow would be better."

"I'll drive over to your place after supper tomorrow, pick her up so she'll be back home in time to get ready for the 4-H show." Mary Jane ruffled Sarah's hair affectionately as she spoke. If Heather was going to spend the day with Sarah tomorrow, both Mary Jane and I had to plan our schedules and adjust our chores.

"Sarah?" I looked at her.

Sarah wasn't stupid. She knew that having Heather over tomorrow was the best she was going to get.

"Okay," she said. Then, belatedly, "Thanks."

"No problem," Mary Jane said.

"About this time tomorrow then, okay?" I asked.

Mary Jane and Heather nodded. "Thank you," Heather said quietly.

I glanced at my watch. "Hurry then, Tiger. I've got to get lunch on and you can help me." Sarah darted back into the house, with Heather behind her. Mary Jane and I stood in the sunshine on her back porch and talked while the girls fetched Sarah's overnight kit, all her 4-H records and her project material.

Mary Jane swatted at a wasp and looked out over the meadow in the centre of the village. "Everything okay at your place?"

"Yeah. The hay's almost in," I said. "One of the calves got into some poison, but it didn't die. What about you? Is everything okay here?"

"We have a different kind of trouble: dirt bikers cutting fences and leaving gates open. Happens every summer, but it seems worse this year."

"We have a little of that too. They cut a couple of fences near the old mill site last week. The dirt bikers like to come in, spin out and do jumps into the soft sawdust. We never seem to be able to catch them, just see the damage they do."

Mary Jane looked away again and I waited. Then she said, "What was the poison?"

"The vet says it's *Wipe Out*, that dewormer. Have you had any problems with it?"

"No poisoning. No. The calves are all right. Tell me about it."

So I told her what I knew about its effect on calves and what the vet gave to counteract it. She listened and I know she memorized everything I said to report to Alphonse later. Information like this goes around the country as fast as we can get it moving.

Heather and Sarah pushed open the screen door and came out carrying Sarah's knapsack and books. Heather spoke to Sarah as if she, Heather, were at least two years older. "Don't forget to write in all your feed supplies or your records won't be complete and you'll lose marks for the club."

Mary Jane smiled at me over Heather's head. They were so serious about their projects.

"Okay. I will. I promise." Sarah waved and ran to the truck. We had one more stop on the Reserve — Silas Man distributes all the mail from his store — then we were off on the rest of our circuit.

"You can choose the tape, Sarah." She picked some soft rock from my collection. I cranked up the sound and we sang "Sweet Dreams Are Made of These" and "I Don't Care What You Say This is My Life" at the top of our voices, with Sarah's arm out the window thumping the rhythm on the side of the truck. Having Sarah with me made it easier to deliver the mail. She either leaned out the passenger-side window and put the mail in, or she hopped out and did it. I didn't have to leave the truck, and we scooted over those twenty miles quickly.

I hit the accelerator the last five miles and braked in the yard at 11:30. Sarah snapped her seat belt open and escaped the truck as if it were on fire.

"Where are you going?"

She whirled around and almost danced on the spot. "To see if Pansy missed me. I bet she was upset this morning when I wasn't there."

I stepped out of the truck. "Devastated," I said, "but she recovered. Come on, Sarah, she'll live through it. Get back here and take your things into the house. I promise you can see Pansy after lunch, but I have work to do and I need you." I also needed to know where Sarah was most of the time so I didn't have to pick her off a rafter or haul her out of the lake.

Sarah hesitated, looked at the barn and then back at me.

I started toward the house and said in the firmest voice

I could find, "Come on."

She came. "You're a bit like a teacher, you know."

A worse insult she couldn't imagine. I glanced at her. "Give me a break, Sarah."

She hurried to keep up with me, her arms full of books. I carried her knapsack. "Well, you're bossy. I bet the boys think so too. That's why you don't have any dates."

"I have some dates."

"One a year." Sarah wanted to make me sorry I'd "bossed" her.

My dating life was almost as bad as Sarah thought. We lived ten miles out of town, and most guys didn't want to drive that far. Sometimes I stayed in town with a girlfriend for the weekend, and dated and went to parties then, but if Sarah thought I wasn't living a typical Hollywood teen-aged life, she was right. I have had exactly four real dates in my entire life. I was probably the only sixteen-year-old in the world who was so inexperienced. No wonder I didn't understand guys; I didn't have any opportunity. Either I lived too far from town or I wasn't attractive to guys, or I didn't have a clue about this male-female thing . . . or all of that.

I hauled out the meatloaf filling that had been thawing in the fridge since yesterday and four loaves of bread from the freezer.

"What smells so good?" Sarah said as she returned from dumping her clothes and her 4-H project in her room.

"Chili for tonight. Listen. The menu for lunch is sand-wiches, apples and carrot cake. Oh, my God! It's frozen solid. I forgot about it."

"I'll get it," Sarah said. "Let's nuke it."

"Okay. The microwave. Good idea." I continued to read the list to the last item. "What do you want to do?"

"I'll wash the apples. You make the sandwiches."

We worked steadily for forty minutes, making enough

sandwiches for ten. I remembered to start the coffee urn. The men came in happy because the haying was almost finished. They took their apples back to the fields with them and left Sarah and me with the dishes.

She told me about her 4-H records and the display she and Heather were making on noxious weeds of the Cariboo, and I told her about my demonstration project on self-defense, which I was doing for my part of the 4-H exhibition on the weekend.

The phone rang twice. Andy Foster called. He's Trevor's dad, and a persistent real estate salesman who phones Dad every two weeks or so. I could picture Mr. Foster, short, bald and red-faced — so unlike Trevor, who is teen-magazine material.

An RCMP constable called wanting to know if Dad or Mom were in. He said he'd either phone back at seven or come out to the ranch. Sarah and I made up stories about what the constable wanted, the sillier the better. There was buried treasure on our property and the police had just found out about it. There was a werewolf loose and they wanted to warn us. Sarah's grade four class had taken over the far meadow and the police needed us to talk them into leaving. Sarah's stories were better than mine. She told me a long one that involved invisible alien police and rock stars.

Dad arrived with the crew at six. All the hay was under cover in the hay sheds and everyone was feeling good about beating the rain. Dad picked up Sarah and waltzed her around the kitchen. I gave him the phone messages.

He snorted when I told him Andy Foster had phoned. "That man can't understand 'No.'"

"What does he want? The same thing?" I opened the oven door and put the ladle in the chili.

"Yeah, the same thing. He wants me to sell the lakeside property to him. 'Great real estate potential.'" Dad sounded just like Andy, pompous and condescending. "Great grassland too, and with water rights. I'm not selling."

The men were happy with the supper, but I was glad to see them all leave. As far as I was concerned, we could live on leftover ham and whatever was in the freezer until Mom came home.

Mom phoned about seven. Sarah answered and talked to her for ten minutes, telling her all about her problems with her 4-H records and how unfair it was to expect her to write everything down. I could see Dad was trying to be patient and let Sarah talk, so I just shook my head when he offered me the phone.

He smiled at me. "I'll talk to her from the bedroom, Karen. Hang this up for me, will you?"

I nodded, waited until I heard the click of the bedroom receiver and then let it drop. The front doorbell rang and Sarah ran to answer it. No one used the front door, so it stuck. I helped her yank it open to let the RCMP constable in.

"Constable Fraser," he said.

"Hi. I'm Karen. This is Sarah. Come on in. Dad's on the phone. Do you want coffee?" I put my shoulder against the door until I heard the latch click.

"Sure, I'd like coffee. Thanks."

He followed Sarah and me into the kitchen and sat at the table. I put a cup of coffee in front of him. Sarah stood on the opposite side, staring at him.

"Sarah, is there any cake left from supper?"

"Yeah." She fetched it from the pantry.

"Have you eaten?" I asked, and only then really looked at him. He was about twenty-five, a little taller than Dad, blue eyes, blond hair and a jagged red scar on the left side of his face.

"No, uh, I was going to eat when I got back to town." He put his hat on the table beside him and passed his hand over his forehead. He smiled at Sarah, but he looked tired.

"Chili okay?" I headed for the oven.

"Great." I heard the chair creak as Constable Fraser leaned back.

The chili was still baking because I had forgotten all about it. I dished out the last of it and added a nuked roll from the freezer and a couple of slices of ham from the fridge.

"Thanks." This time, *I* got the smile.

"Go ahead. Dad's on the phone. He'll be awhile." I put the chili pan to soak while Sarah sat with Constable Fraser.

"Do you want some pickles?" I heard her ask. She had picked up his hat and was fingering the insignia.

"No, thanks. This is fine. Great, in fact." He ate quickly as if he might have to leave before he could finish.

"Good. Were you starving?" Sarah still watched him like a visitor examining a new zoo resident.

"Just starving," he agreed. At least he seemed amused by Sarah and not offended.

"How did you get that scar?" Trust Sarah to be blunt. There wasn't any sense in telling her not to ask. She was going to ask and Mom said that she'd learn not to hurt others. It didn't seem to bother Constable Fraser.

"I wasn't very smart about trying to stop a fight and I got between a man and a broken bottle." He fingered the scar lightly, then shrugged.

"Did you learn anything?" Sarah asked.

The constable looked at Sarah with more interest. "You bet," he said. "I'll tell you, Sarah. Take it from me. Here is one of the truths of life: never try to take away someone's broken bottle."

Sarah smiled, delighted that an adult was paying her attention. "You're kidding, right?"

I brought a cup of coffee to the table for myself. "Of course, he's kidding. Come on, Sarah. Lay off." I turned to him. "So, Constable, what brings you here?"

"Butt out, Karen," Sarah objected. "It wasn't your conversation."

I felt heat flood my face. She was right. Exasperating, picky, irritating, but right. I shouldn't have interfered in her conversation. I took a deep breath. "Okay. I'm sorry."

The constable watched us, his eyes twinkling, too polite to laugh at our bickering. He finished the last of the chili. "Uh, Will," he said. "My name's Will."

I still was embarrassed to be caught quarrelling with a ten-year-old. Inept, that's what I was, socially inept. I tried again. "So tell us, Will, what's the problem?"

He reached for his coffee and hesitated. Maybe he didn't talk to anyone under forty; then he made up his mind. "We got a report from a vet that a lot of ranchers are losing calves."

"Reena. Organophosphate poisoning. *Wipe Out*."

"Right. You lose any?" His eyes narrowed and he was suddenly more alert.

"No. We had a case yesterday, but Reena saved the calf. We didn't find the *Wipe Out*, though, and that means another calf might get it." That worried me. I didn't want any calf to suffer the seizures I'd seen yesterday, and I sure didn't want any of *my* calves to die.

Constable Will Fraser stirred his coffee and stared at it for a moment. "The vet thought all those calves in one area was so unusual that she reported it to us."

Police. Crime. Evil. Danger. Thoughts spun quickly through my head. Why the police and not someone from the Department of Agriculture? "As a criminal problem? In case it was deliberate?"

He nodded. He was used to crime, wicked people doing ugly things. Other than a few snaky girls at school, I wasn't used to it, and I needed to know more. "How many is Reena talking about?"

"Twelve."

Twelve calves dying in seizures. Twelve cows bawling for their calves. It *was* criminal. "We didn't know it was that many, but we knew it was more than seemed accidental."

Dad came out of the bedroom right then. The constable introduced himself and told Dad why he was there. Dad fetched a cup of coffee and sat down with us. "Can't see why, though," he said.

"Twelve calves are worth quite a lot of money, aren't they?" The constable tried to see the problem more clearly.

Dad was willing to give what information he could. "Twelve calves among twelve ranches isn't a problem. Twelve calves on one ranch would be. You a ranch boy, Constable?"

"Will," he said. "Will Fraser. And no. I'm from Toronto."

"Okay then, I'll tell you how it works." Dad turned and picked up a pencil and paper from the counter and wrote as he spoke. "I feed a cow for a year to produce one calf, and then I feed that calf for eighteen months before I sell it. If it dies, I'm not only out the money I spent on its mother for a year, but I'm out the sale of that calf eighteen months later. I have to wait another year for another calf, and another eighteen months to sell it." He added up the costs and underlined the total. "So I lose time and I lose money. I'm in the business of raising calves. If they die, I'm not in business. Twelve dead calves wouldn't break me, but it would hurt and . . . ." He paused. "It's ugly."

"Would you say that the fact that twelve calves were poisoned by *Wipe Out* is unusual?"

I glared at him. *I* told him it was; *Reena* told him it was. How many people did he have to ask before he believed it?

"Yeah. Unusual and cruel to the calves. They should be protected from a crazy who is going around killing them." I saw Dad's fingers tighten on the pencil.

"But losing calves wouldn't put you out of business?"

"Not for a couple of years." Dad shook his head. "Losing hay might."

Constable Fraser looked interested.

Dad continued. "We had a bad crop last year — rain

and freeze-up too early, so I had to buy hay. I had already borrowed money to buy that strip of property along the lake, then I had to borrow to buy the hay. If the hay hadn't been good this year, I would have had to buy hay again and that might have forced me into selling cattle or," he added as an afterthought, "the lake property, depending on the price of hay and the deal I could make at the bank."

"But you got all your hay in?" the constable asked.

"All under cover," Dad said with satisfaction. "Let it rain."

The constable nodded, then was silent for a moment while he thought. "So, dying calves is a sad fact, but not a financially disastrous one?"

"It's not disastrous right now," Dad said, "but the cows are on summer range. Some of them are in the bush and we won't see them until the fall. If someone is deliberately spreading poison around, it might kill more than twelve calves — a lot more."

We were all quiet for a moment. I imagined calves dying under the trees, down in ravines or beside the lake. We had a thousand acres of government range land as well as a thousand of our own. If calves were dying in the bush, it would take us weeks to find them all.

"Something seems to be organized behind the calf poisonings. There are too many to be random or coincidental. I'm looking for motives and I can't seem to find any, but I don't believe in coincidences. Maybe you could talk to other ranchers and let me know if there's anything I should be looking for." The constable stood to indicate he was finished.

"I'll do that. Thanks for coming." The ranchers might get together and figure out what was happening to the calves, and they might or might not tell the police. They have ways of their own to discourage strangers from causing harm on the ranches.

"No problem. Thanks for supper." He nodded at me and at Sarah.

Sarah smiled. "Go out the back way," she said. "No one uses the front door." I guessed Sarah had decided to adopt Constable Will Fraser as her friend. She bounced up and offered him her hand to shake as if she were the hostess.

Constable Fraser shook it solemnly. "I'll remember that next time." He shook hands with Dad and with me, then left. Dad walked out with him, while Sarah and I piled the dishes in the dishwasher and turned it on.

Dad ran his fingers through his hair as he came back into the room. "Your mother wanted to know how you were making out, Karen, and I told her you were doing great."

"Thanks, Dad." His red hair stood up on his head, hay stuck in his shirt pocket, grease streaked his jeans and somehow he didn't seem as tall as usual.

"Well, you are doing great, but I wish she were here." He turned then and stood at the window looking out at the lake. He didn't like Mom to be away, but he never told her not to go.

"Grandma needs her." I stood beside him. The air was still and the late evening sky glimmered in the lake, pale yellow and deep blues reflecting the light and dark patterns of clouds.

"Yeah. She needs her, but she doesn't appreciate her. She's a bit of a witch, that Mrs. MacRae."

I'd never heard Dad talk that way about Grandma. She lives far enough away that we don't see her much, but I hadn't realized Dad didn't like her. I stared at him.

He shrugged. "She doesn't treat your mother very well," he said. "I don't like her to stay there long."

I watched him for a moment, not really understanding his mood.

He shrugged again. "I'm getting my pipes."

He meant that he was going to play his bagpipes.

"I'm going down to the dock," I said quickly.

"I'll go with you," Sarah chimed in. We left before Dad inflated the pipes. We both liked them, but we didn't like them too close to us. We ran across the grass and sat on the dock with our bare feet hanging in the water.

It was almost dark. A fish plopped not far out. A bird, probably a kingfisher, darted past us, skimmed the water and was gone. Lights from Kevin's place twinkled halfway down the lake, and the Jennings' lights were faint at the far end. I heard a rustle in the grass, one of the dogs, Pinto or Jock, looking for mice. They worked with the cattle most days and stayed with Dad, responding to his directions. They didn't have much time to play or go off on their own business. I could see the white patches on its coat, the black blended into the grass.

Dad must have been in the meadow near the barn because we heard Pansy complain when the first drone wailed. Then the second and third drones filled out the sound until he had a harmonic base to his chanter. He played a sad song, what he calls a lament, haunting and, in a way, beautiful coming to us over the grass and drifting off over the lake into the night. Sarah edged closer to me until I pulled her onto my lap.

She turned and snuggled, holding me around the waist and laying her head on my chest. "Your heart sounds like a drum," she said.

I hugged her. We sat like that for a long time, while Dad played songs about loneliness and worry. Then the tunes changed a little, became quicker, lighter somehow. Sarah fidgeted and pushed away. She clambered to her feet when Dad switched to a fast-stepping reel and said, "Challenge!"

I had taught her a game when she was a toddler: I did a step and she tried to copy me. Now she turned the game on me and did a fast dance step.

I scrambled to my feet. "No fair. I didn't see it. Do it again."

She did it again, then waited. I did what I thought she had done.

"Right," she said. "Try this." She did another.

Dad came closer, still playing, until he was at the end of the dock giving us fast reels and dance steps. Sarah and I danced the steps we'd learned at dance class and new ones we'd invented. We danced faster and faster and wilder and wilder, whooping and shouting and stamping our feet on the dock.

Suddenly the music stopped, and the sound died in a slow, wheezing wail. I lay flat on the dock with Sarah collapsed on top of me, our breathing hard and rapid. In a few minutes we were breathing quietly, but we lay there listening to the silence of the night. Then a loon called, wild and clear as if he were a spirit from another world. The high notes fell into the darkening night air like loneliness. There's a real world out there, Kevin had said. What did he mean? A world of feelings? I hugged Sarah closer and let the night come.

Chapter 3

The next morning I picked up Heather from her house so she could spend the day with Sarah and finished the mail route quickly with their help. When we returned home, the two of them closeted themselves in Sarah's room, completing their 4-H records with only murmurs and occasional giggles to tell me they were working.

I had a 4-H project of my own to get ready, a demonstration on three karate self-defense moves. I had to make sure my *gi*, my white karate uniform, was clean and pressed and that both my 4-H shirt and Sarah's were ready for tomorrow's exhibition.

I stood in the basement laundry room ironing my *gi*, the white material draped over the ironing board and hanging down to the floor. Through the low window I could see grass, shrubs, the dock and the lake beyond. Water hemlock and purple asters swayed slightly in the breeze beside the dock. A mallard nibbled at the weeds near the shore.

Without warning, a battalion of five grebes burst from the tall grass, charged into the lake, changed direction with the precision of a gymnastics team, then anxiously paddled out of sight. Maybe a coyote or a fox had scared them, or they had responded to some crazy, internal fright; grebes panic easily, rushing off to get away from nothing in particular. The sun glinted on the water; the air was warm. For a moment I felt lazy and comfortable. I shook myself. I didn't have time to stare at the lake and drift around in my thoughts.

I mentally rehearsed my karate demonstration project. The idea was to explain self-defense moves to the audience while demonstrating them. My best friend Paula had agreed to be my partner and act as my mugger if I promised not to hurt her. I'd promised. Now I needed to make sure that the moves I demonstrated would be clearly seen by the audience, that I wouldn't injure Paula, and that I remembered what to say and when to say it.

I'd carried my information cards with me all week so I could memorize them. They were, at this moment, propped on the end of the ironing board. I reread them, trying to think about the public-speaking hints my 4-H leader had given me. "Be precise. Be audible and look interested in your own information." I wasn't a karate expert — I just had an orange belt — but our instructor taught the self-defense, mugger-breaking moves early in our course. "Tell your audience not to be afraid to hurt their attacker," she had told me. "He is certainly going to hurt them."

It was surprisingly hard to make myself deliberately hurt another person even at karate class, where trying to hurt another person was part of the lesson. Kevin took karate with me. We sometimes practised side by side, but never on each other. I couldn't bring myself to hit him. I'm not sure why. I managed to hit my instructor a few times and a couple of other kids in my class, but I couldn't hit Kevin. He never tried to attack me either. We didn't talk about it; we just avoided each other in class.

I had been idly moving from thought to thought, ignoring the present, but now I was aware of increasing tension in the back of my neck and along my shoulders. It got stronger. I knew what was coming. I hadn't had a feeling like this for a couple of years, but I knew what it was. I stared straight ahead as the walls of the laundry room seemed to blur and move away from me. The hairs on my arms prickled and my breathing grew rapid. I felt an overwhelming sense of confusion and anger. Emotions washed over me and then through me. These weren't my feelings; they were Kevin's. I knew they were Kevin's. He was sending me a message, a thought force, a psychic blast, and I didn't want to know it. I hated this invasion of my brain. I felt as if I was being drowned in his feelings, and I couldn't escape.

A wave of turbulence came from him, not anger exactly, but emotion of some kind, rolling, sparking, roaring through me. It lasted only a few seconds. One part of me acted normally. I stopped ironing, and stood still, while most of my concentration was on what I was feeling. It had to be Kevin. I didn't like this. It was uncomfortable and unreasonable. I liked methodical thinking, analytical paths of deduction, mathematical certainty, not this powerful, uncontrollable sensation.

Kevin and I used to be able to send feelings this way when we were younger, but we hadn't done it for years. We had stopped wanting to know each other that well when I was about fourteen. I had blocked him out and he must have done the same. I had tried to ignore what he was feeling yesterday and today. It wasn't going to work. He was getting through. Something was wrong. Kevin was full of some kind of emotion and upset by it, really upset. If he was in trouble, I had to talk to him.

I unplugged the iron and sank onto the sofa. I dialled his number on the basement phone.

"He just headed over to your house, Karen," his mother said. "In his truck, not in the boat. I thought you had called him."

"No, I didn't phone," I said, "but I'll look for him."

"Fine. See you tomorrow at the show."

I hung up and stared at the empty TV screen for a moment. Kevin was sending me a message through ESP, super sense, psychic dimension or whatever it's called.

We're not crazy. People do have an extra sense at times. Mom said her aunt had been that way, but it is a little weird. It makes me feel different from others. If I had to have a sixth sense, why couldn't I be receptive to my mom's or dad's feelings, or somebody else's? Why Kevin's?

I walked out into the yard to wait. If Kevin was as agitated as I thought he was, he wouldn't want to talk in the house where Sarah could hear him.

He pulled in the yard scattering gravel with his skidding stop and threw open the passenger door. "Get in! The dirt bikers are in the north pasture. I saw them as I was driving in. If we move fast, we might catch them."

This wasn't what I had been expecting. This wasn't what he was upset about, was it? Dirt bikers! I thought quickly. "Do you have a phone with you?"

He nodded. I jumped in and fastened my seat belt as he put the truck into gear. I grabbed his phone and dialled the house.

Sarah answered.

"Sarah, it's Karen. Listen. I'm going to the north pasture to try to catch some dirt bikers. I'm with Kevin. You and Heather will be alone for about a half-hour, okay?"

"No problem," she said. "Are you going to shoot them?" Sarah liked direct action.

"No. I'll talk to you later. Bye." I hung up and immediately dialled Dad.

He answered on the first ring. I knew he was checking fence lines, so I felt lucky that he wasn't away from his truck, down a gully pounding staples into a post. I told him where Kevin and I were going and why.

"I've got Lyle and Mike with me," Dad said. "We'll meet you in the north pasture. Wait for us before you do anything."

"Okay."

I hung up, and then hung on as Kevin left the road

and went across the fields. We bounced over the rough hay meadows and then travelled more smoothly over the dirt trail through the woods, but hit potholes often enough to make me glad I was wearing a seat belt. I could see the north pasture through a gap in the trees, but it was only as we broke through the screen of the poplar and birch and rolled through the gate to the big field that I saw the bikers.

There were two of them on dirt bikes harassing a herd of about twenty cows and ten calves. The bikers were dressed alike in grey, one-piece bike suits with black helmets that included over-the-face smoked black visors, looking like a hundred faceless bad guys in the movies I'd seen. As I watched, one of them drove toward a big cow. She bawled and tried to pivot on her back legs to get away from him. He stopped inches from her, the bike engine revved high. The cow called again in confusion. The biker pulled back, turned and started toward another cow. He looked up then and saw us. He braked and held his bike still, the front wheels about a foot off the ground, the bike balanced by his grip on the handlebars and his stiff-legged stance. Dad's truck burst through the second open gate; Mike's was right behind him. Mike's truck, with Mr. Jennings in the passenger seat, immediately started around the outside of the field against the barbed wire.

"He's checking for a break in the fence," I said.

"Yeah." Kevin put the truck in reverse, backed up and stopped in the gateway. "I'll block this gate. Your dad's got the other. Mike will put his truck in front of any hole in the fence." Mike stopped his truck directly opposite us.

Everyone got out of the trucks — four men, me and the two dogs Dad had with him. The bikers looked at us and slowly turned their bikes, moving closer to each other. They had stopped in front of a small pond, so their escape had to be toward us or to either side.

The cows were accustomed to the noise of motors — we

used the tractor to move hay around them all winter — but they didn't like the way the bikes had come so close to them. They moved around the bikers, unsure of where to go or what to do. Cows won't run far unless they are forced to. They usually run a few steps then stop. I've always wondered how film directors get the cows to stampede in western movies.

Cows are not smart; dogs are. Dad's whistles sent the dogs in a circle around the cows. Pinto and Jock had been working cattle since they were pups. They darted and shifted in mercurial motion until they forced the cows into a semi-circle in front of the bikers. The cows were confused and started to move away, but the dogs barked and spun, keeping them from breaking out. Cows don't move very fast, at least not usually, and would rather bunch than act independently.

We walked toward the bikes. Dad whistled more instructions to the dogs. Pinto cut out a group of five cows and drove them away while Jock kept the rest together. We moved closer, Dad directing the dogs until slowly they reduced the herd to about ten cows that jostled, bellowed and moved anxiously in front of the bikes. The bikers didn't have room to gather speed and couldn't push their bikes through the thousands of pounds of beef.

Dad left the dogs maintaining the formation, stepping around the cows as he headed for the two helmeted boys on the bikes. The rest of us slipped quietly around and between the cows, slapping them on their rumps, ducking under their necks, always getting closer until the bikers were backed against the pond by four men, me and the shifting cows.

Dad reached over and jerked the keys out of the ignition on the nearest bike. Mr. Jennings did the same to the other. The boys started to grab for their keys, but changed their minds when they saw how close and menacing the men were. Dad whistled to the dogs and the cows started to move away.

"Off the bikes, fellows," Dad said quietly.

"No way. Give us our keys," the taller one said.

Kevin grabbed the handlebars of the taller one's bike and jerked. Mike did the same to the other bike. The bikers got off.

"Those are our bikes, man. You can get charged for stealing," the tallest one tried to threaten Dad, but his voice lost power and came out almost a croak.

"Helmets off, boys," Dad said, crowding a little closer. Mr. Jennings moved up beside him.

"We weren't really going to hurt any of those cows, we were just seeing how close we. . . . "

Mr. Jennings reached over, pulled the snap and yanked the helmet off the boy who was speaking. The other boy slowly reached up and took off his own helmet.

The tallest one was Trevor Foster, dark-eyed, intense Trevor. I stared at him. This was the guy I had fantasies about? The one I wanted to date? No taste, Karen, I told myself. You just can't pick them. He was sophisticated, smooth, fun and sexy. A catalogue of my previous ideas about him flipped like a library card file through my mind.

The shorter one was Bob MacRae, sixteen, in grade ten, easygoing, always a follower. I could understand how he would blunder into trouble.

Trevor had been looking at the men and now suddenly stared at me. I flushed and looked away. I was embarrassed. Why was *I* embarrassed? I hadn't done anything wrong.

"Into the back of the pickup," Dad said. "You can explain yourself to the RCMP."

"I wasn't doing anything. Just fooling around." Trevor's voice was sharp. He stood straight, as if he were willing to fight everyone at once. "I've got my rights, man." The men were grim-faced and angry, and they were bigger and much stronger than Trevor. When they crowded him, he seemed to sag, and moved toward Dad's truck. He stopped there and turned to me. "Come on, Karen. Tell them I wasn't going to hurt anything."

There wasn't a chance of that. I didn't even want to. "Get real, Trevor. Three of those cows are mine. "

Mr. Jennings crowded him, and Trevor climbed into the back of the truck. Dad followed him.

"Karen, you drive my truck," Dad said. "Mike, you and Kevin come with me and these juvenile delinquents here. Lyle, you load their bikes and take them downtown to the detachment. Use Kevin's truck. We'll come back for Mike's truck later. We have to fix the fence anyway."

Everyone moved to do as Dad directed. Kevin shoved the silent Bob MacRae after Trevor into the back of Dad's truck. Bob's eyes had widened when he had seen the men standing close to him earlier, and he hadn't said a word to provoke them. I think the RCMP looked like safety and comfort compared to the four men crowding him.

Trevor was arguing and threatening legal action again —and I had thought Trevor was smart. "My dad will have you in court. You can't take our bikes or our helmets. The RCMP won't have a charge against us. Trespassing is the best you can do and we can pay that fine easy."

"You're telling us true, are you?" Dad said mildly. "You just might be right about that." He looked over at Mr. Jennings. "Seems a shame to have you get away with a fine."

Mr. Jennings nodded.

Dad told me to get into the truck and drive, but to hand him the phone first. I saw him talking on it as I drove back to the house, so I wasn't surprised to see the RCMP vehicle drive in right behind us. Will Fraser was the cop on patrol.

He listened to Dad's report of the boys' harassing the cattle. Kevin added the fact that fence had been cut. Will told Trevor and Bob they had a right to remain silent, but Trevor defended himself. He denied they had cut the fence and he denied that they were harassing the cattle. Bob MacRae just shook his head when Will asked him for his account.

"I'll take them into the detachment," Will said, "and call their parents."

"I want my bike back," Trevor demanded. His curly hair fell over his forehead and his dark eyes looked defiant and frightened at the same time. What did he expect to happen when he started this trouble?

"Mr. Jennings will leave them at the RCMP detachment," Dad said. "The RCMP can give them to you."

"They'd better." If he'd been young, fourteen instead of seventeen, I would have thought he was only stupid. But he was six foot two, muscular and only caught today because there had been four men out there in the field. It wasn't easy to think of him as a stupid kid; he was a man, really.

"I don't know why you'd want it back." Dad rocked back on his heels and levelled a look at Trevor. "It didn't look to be in very good shape."

I remembered the gleaming chrome, the maroon and black polished paint. I glanced sideways at Dad.

"It was in great shape," Trevor responded quickly.

"No, it wasn't. I'd be ashamed to own dinged-up equipment like that. You should take better care of it."

Trevor started to protest and then stopped and stared at Dad.

Will's radio squawked and he reached into his squad car and answered the call. He was now a little distance from us.

"Yeah," Kevin said quietly to Trevor. "You ride a piece of junk."

Trevor looked from Dad to Kevin then back to Dad. "You wouldn't. . . . " he started, and then his voice died.

"Well, now," Dad said evenly. "Why wouldn't I? Did you think you could do whatever you wanted and never pay for it?"

Trevor was silent for moment. Will pushed Trevor toward the cruiser. "*You'll* pay," Trevor said, shrugging away from Will. He looked around angrily, saw me and said, "I'll see you at school, Karen. Count on it," before Will bundled him and Bob into the back seat of the cruiser.

Trevor didn't look quite so threatening without his helmet, but he was taller than me and stronger. I tried to remember whether Trevor was part of any gang or had a bunch of dangerous friends. I didn't think so. He usually had a girlfriend or hung around with younger kids, but he *had* just threatened me. Maybe I'd better practise my karate. I wasn't so blind to other people's emotions that I didn't recognize anger and vindictiveness when they slapped me in the face.

Will put his car in gear and rolled down his window to speak to Dad. "I'll let you know what happens. And I appreciate you bringing them in instead of dealing with them in your field."

Some ranchers would have beat them. I knew that. They got angry when kids ruined fences and caused damage, when their parents didn't make any effort to prevent them from doing damage and when the courts didn't punish them.

"I believe in justice," Dad said. Will looked at him sharply, but only nodded. We watched the squad car leave the ranch.

Sarah and Heather had been hanging out the window and now wanted a play-by-play of the great capture. Dad picked up some fencing tools and he, Kevin and Mike went back to the north pasture to fix the fence.

I started supper and explained what had happened to Heather and Sarah and again to Mary Jane when she came to pick up Heather.

"I'm glad someone caught them," Mary Jane said. "They're probably the same kids who have been bothering our cattle."

"It was Trevor Foster," I said. "I have a hard time believing I really saw him do it. He's such a neat guy at school."

"I guess you didn't know him very well." Mary Jane fished in her purse for her truck keys.

"I thought I did."

"You might be like Heather," Mary Jane said. "She thinks people only act from their head."

I thought about that after she left. I didn't know Trevor very well, but he wasn't a total jerk. I'd seen him act with kindness to Joanne, a girl in our class who was a little slower than most. And I remembered the fun we'd had together when we decorated for the grade eleven dance last year. I had a hard time putting that Trevor together with this Trevor.

And what did Mary Jane mean, I thought people only acted from their heads? I knew people had emotions like anger and fear and sexual desire, but I didn't think they should necessarily act on them all the time. Emotions are irrational. People *shouldn't* act on them, most of the time. But then, what did I know?

The men came in for supper. Naturally. Everyone always eats at our house. Mr. Jennings returned from town at the same time. I put spaghetti on the table and the meal was almost over before anyone asked Mr. Jennings if he'd dropped off the bikes at the RCMP office.

"Yeah," he said. "I just left them in the alley around the back. Should be pretty easy to find."

"They might get hit by a car out there," Mike said.

"Yeah," Mr. Jennings said, "I think they did get hit," and went back to eating. There was a moment's silence. No one really wanted to ask Mr. Jennings what he had done.

Kevin changed the subject to new haying equipment and no one spoke again about the bikes.

We had finished dinner and were sitting around with coffee when the dogs announced a visitor. Sarah bounced up to check the back door and returned with Bryan Tyeson, the bank manager from town.

"How's it going, Bryan?" Dad said. "Want coffee?"

Tyeson was a tall man, bald with a fringe of grey hair around his ears, bright blue eyes, and probably as old as Dad. He was one of the few people I'd met whose eyes really twinkled, as if they had electric sparks tumbling through them.

"Thanks. I'd like that." He smiled at the men and then stared at me. "And who is this?" He turned to Dad.

"Karen, this is Bryan Tyeson. Bryan, my daughter, Karen." Dad waved his hand at me.

"I've met you before, Mr. Tyeson," I said. "Would you like coffee?"

"Sure. Sure." He hung his Stetson on the knob of the chair. "I can't believe I'd forget you. How's everyone today?"

The men nodded. It was hard not to respond in a friendly way to Bryan Tyeson, even when he annoyed you. He was like a Labrador puppy: cheerful, happy and a little awkward.

He sat at the table while I brought him coffee.

"I thought I'd stop by and see how your season went." Tyeson accepted the coffee and nodded his thanks.

"Want to make sure your payment's going to come in next week?" Dad handed Sarah a plate of brownies. She took one and passed them on.

"No real fear you'll renege. I just thought I'd check to see if your haying was going well and, of course, that you would be able to bring me a nice, fat payment on the loan."

At that, the other men rose to leave, grabbing brownies off the plate on their way out. Bank talk was private. In my house, bank talk was *family* talk, so I stayed to listen.

"No problem," Dad said. "I had a good hay crop and it's all under cover."

Tyeson's face grew serious and he leaned forward. "I heard you were having trouble. Losing calves, someone said."

He nodded at the men as they left and smiled politely at Sarah, then ignored her. Sarah rolled her eyes at me from behind his back. Tyeson hadn't given her any special attention and she didn't like that. I'd heard he had lost his ten-year-old son in a car accident several years ago. His wife, Lydia, had been driving — drunk, people said. Maybe he survived the pain of all that by ignoring children.

Dad answered him. "Yeah. It's pretty bad, but it isn't going to hurt us financially. The only thing that might have done that was a bad hay crop. Two years in a row of poor hay might have forced me to sell something. But we're okay now and probably never again will be as vulnerable to a financial crisis as we were this year."

"Good planning, Dan. You sure stay on top of your production."

"Not everything goes according to plan," Dad said. "Some things are unpredictable — like rain."

"No," Bryan Tyeson disagreed. "You plan for rain. Everything about this operation is well planned."

Kevin returned to the kitchen. "Excuse me, but I'd like to talk to Karen for a moment."

I looked up in surprise, but followed him to the back door.

Sarah called me from her room. "Karen, I can't make these records balance. Will you help me?"

"In a minute, Sarah." I slipped out onto the porch.

Kevin stood at the door, looking out over the lake. A couple of boats were anchored at the far end; a few people were fishing. A loon called, wildly proclaiming ownership of the bay.

"What is it, Kevin?" Then I remembered the strong feelings I'd picked up from him that afternoon. "This isn't just about the bikers, is it? Something else is bothering you."

"Yeah." He turned suddenly. "Why? Did you sense me?"

Sarah came to the door. "Karen, I *really* need your help. Heather's going to kill me if I mess this up."

"I'll be there in a minute, Sarah. Go on back to your room. I promise, as soon as Kevin leaves, I'll be there."

She looked at Kevin, but didn't tell him to leave right now. "All right."

I turned back to Kevin when Sarah closed the door. "Yes, I felt you."

"What was it like?"

"You were upset about something. A little angry."

He laughed softly. "I was frustrated." He looked past me. "You've got me frustrated!"

"Me? This isn't my fault. What did I do wrong?"

"Nothing's wrong. Everything's right, great, super even. And I'm leaving town in three weeks." He shoved his hands into his jeans and stared out at the lake again.

"Yeah. I know. You start university. So?"

"Don't you feel anything?"

"What am I supposed to feel? What's the matter?"

He turned back to me and sighed. "Look. Maybe we could talk tomorrow after the dance. You're busy here and I have to get home."

"Whatever." I wasn't the one with the problem.

He suddenly grabbed my shoulder to prevent me from turning.

I looked at him. I did feel something then, a tingling where his hand gripped my shoulder, an expectancy, an excitement.

He must have seen something in my eyes because he smiled down at me. Whatever had been bothering him before didn't seem to be upsetting him now. He ran his finger along my cheek. I stared at him. He seemed different — taller, older, a little remote. It was as if he saw something I didn't. I didn't feel like a girlfriend being pursued by a boyfriend. I felt like Karen being treated like a child by Kevin. That annoyed me. If he knew something I didn't, I wanted to hear about it. I was suddenly angry.

"What is it?" I said sharply, drawing back.

"Karen!" Sarah's patience was exhausted. She shouted through the window, "Come *on!*"

The back door opened behind me and Dad and Bryan Tyeson walked onto the porch. Everyone, including Kevin, said good night, and I went in to help Sarah. It took a half-hour to deal with Sarah's problems, and I still had to iron our shirts and get my demonstration ready.

Dad came down to the laundry room to ask if I needed anything for the sale tomorrow. I didn't.

"Dad, what did Mr. Jennings mean about Trevor's bike? Did he wreck it?"

"Probably," Dad said.

"He shouldn't have done that."

It wasn't Mr. Jennings' job to hand out justice to Trevor; that's what police and courts were for. And then I realized that I was glad he had done it. It made me *feel* better. Trevor should pay for harassing the cows with more than a small fine. Could I disapprove of something with my mind yet approve of it with my feelings at the same time?

"No, he shouldn't have wrecked the bike — he probably didn't do much damage, Karen, dented it a little maybe — but people get irritated by useless laws."

"That doesn't mean they should take the law into their own hands."

"No, it doesn't. It seems that the more people there are per acre, the more laws we need; the fewer people, the fewer laws."

I stared at him. "We wouldn't have any environmental

laws if that were so."

"Uh, true." He looked struck by that idea. "Maybe I should say that the fewer the people, the more responsibility each person has to see that justice is done."

"Mr. Jennings shouldn't have wrecked those bikes." I wanted to be sure. Action should be right or wrong, not half-right and a little wrong.

"You're right. He shouldn't have."

Dad left me with the uncomfortable feeling that Mr. Jennings' action was both wrong and right at the same time.

I tried to memorize my information cards, but found myself thinking more about Trevor Foster than about getting first place in the demonstration. Why would he deliberately harass our cows? Was it just our cows or, as Mary Jane thought, was he responsible for all the vandalism on the ranches? Why would someone who had so much going for him waste his time playing "Scare the cows?" It was stupid.

And Kevin. What was so overwhelming that he had to send me a mental message? Us, I suppose. Kevin and Karen. He wants to get into my mind and know me too well. Why couldn't he leave things the way they'd always been? We could be friends. I flipped through the information cards, not really seeing them. Maybe I was wrong and he wanted to talk about something else besides our relationship. Whatever it was, it was emotional and irrational. Mary Jane was probably right. I didn't understand emotion very well.

Chapter 4

"Block that hole!" Dad yelled at me as Sarah's ewe lamb, Pansy, headed for an opening and freedom. Pansy only needed to walk from the back of the truck, across the tailgate and down the ramp of the loading chute, but she seemed determined to jump through the small space between the truck and the chute.

Cows bawled, sheep bleated, kids yelled at their animals and at each other. Trucks were lined up behind us. Adults stood outside their vehicles talking and watching the activity. Everyone needed to unload their 4-H animals at the same time. We didn't want to spend the next ten or twenty minutes chasing Pansy while they waited for us.

I threw out my arms and spread my body across the gap between the truck and the chute. Pansy hesitated when she saw me in her way, changed her mind and jumped from the truck into the chute. Sarah dashed after Pansy, driving her down the narrow, board-lined galley into an empty stall.

"That's it," Dad said as he bolted the gate shut behind her. "Karen, you look after your heifer and Sarah . . . Sarah!" he yelled at her. Sarah had climbed the boards and was now two stalls away, talking to a friend.

"Coming." She responded to the peremptory tone in Dad's voice. Sarah was spoiled, but there were times when even she knew when instant obedience was smart.

"I'm here." She slid off the fence and landed in front of Dad, momentarily still.

"See that you stay here." Dad slammed the tailgate

closed. "Karen has her own work to do; she doesn't have time to follow you around. You look after Pansy: feed, water, tack, supplies, everything tidy and in its place. I'll be back in half an hour and you be right here. Got that, Missy? Right here."

Sarah nodded solemnly. "Right here."

Dad grinned and ruffled her hair. "Okay then." He turned to me. "Do you need anything?"

I mentally listed all the supplies I'd need for the day: my karate demonstration materials, tack for Edie. "No. I'm fine."

"Okay. I'll park the truck, and be back soon."

The cattle barn was busy with adults, kids and animals. I wondered if a beehive felt like this — humming with activity and full of purposeful movement. I'd worked with these people before, known them a long time and been involved in many activities with them. Most of them were my friends. I felt at home, comfortable, as if I belonged.

It took a few minutes for Sarah and me to lead our animals to their designated places. Each club in the Cariboo district had a section throughout the big cattle barn. Our section was the Misty Lake 4-H Club compound, a semi-circular compound with our club sign above the entrance. A wooden plaque on the wall above each animal announced its name, age and weight like an individual business card.

I tied Edie beside two other heifers: Paula Jennings' and Mike Larson's stood beside her. Sarah led Pansy to the wooden sheep pen on the other side of the cows and locked the gate. Bales of hay, eight high and smelling of clover and sunshine, formed a barrier to the public on the other side of the sheep.

As far as I can tell, sheep are psychologically unstable and likely to faint or get sick if you frighten them, or even hurt their feelings, so we needed to protect them from the public. I don't know why Sarah likes them; they're permanent babies and a lot of trouble.

I placed the folding chairs Mr. Jennings had donated between the hay bales and the sheep pens. That way, whenever we had time to sit down, we would be close to the sheep and could protect their precious sensibilities.

In front of each club's compound, members arranged their educational displays so the public and the 4-H judges could examine them, learn from them and come into the compound and ask questions if they wanted more information. Heather brought most of the display that she and Sarah had worked on.

"Put it down right here," I heard Heather say. I moved out in front of the compound. Heather was directing her dad, Alphonse.

"How's it going?" Alphonse grinned at me. He was dressed in town clothes today: black cowboy jeans, white shirt and black Stetson trimmed with a band of red and turquoise beadwork. He had been a champion bareback rider before he married Mary Jane and he still looked like a rodeo athlete.

I answered him. "It's going great. Hi, Mary Jane."

Mary Jane peered out from behind a cardboard box. "Hi, are you organized?"

"I hope so."

Sarah helped Heather place their pictures and typewritten material on the table and on the stand-up cardboard display boards. Mary Jane, Alphonse and I stood back. There was a sign somewhere in the building that cautioned parents not to do the work for their children. Sarah and Heather could be disqualified from competition if adults helped. Club members were allowed to help each other, but because I was older, I wasn't supposed to do much. 4-H teaches "learn by doing," and Sarah and Heather were supposed to do all this themselves.

"Karen! It's about time you got here." Paula Jennings, dark hair bouncing and earrings jangling, grabbed my hand and dragged me back toward the sheep pens. "You won't believe who's here, big as life and six times as handsome."

"Mike?" Paula had recently noticed Mike Larson as an interesting male. She had gone with Allan MacKenna for three years, but she told me once that she and Allan weren't serious. She'd told me she wasn't serious about Mike either, but I wasn't sure I believed her. Paula lived at the end of the lake, and we had ridden the school bus together since grade one. She talked about friends and guys easily, but she had never described Mike as handsome before.

"No, not Mike. Although he's got to be here somewhere because his heifer is. It's someone you're going to want to see."

"Who?" I smiled at her. What was she up to? Paula is always trying to encourage my social development. She says that I need help. Okay, she's right. While I'm always interested in what she has in mind, I'm also cautious.

"Trevor Foster."

My smile faded.

"What's the matter?" Her dark eyes held mine, suddenly serious. "I thought you had your eye on him."

Paula and I usually burn the telephone wires reporting on our lives, but I'd been so busy that I hadn't had a chance to talk to her about Trevor.

"He's trouble, Paula. Morally challenged pond scum." I told her then about the problems we'd been having with vandals, about the RCMP and Trevor. "He's probably going to get some kind of probation or something and he blames me."

"Get real," she said in disbelief. "How could he? He's not stupid." Paula had had math class with Trevor last year.

"No, but he's mad. I was there. I saw him. Believe it; he blames me."

Paula looked worried for a moment, her eyebrows a straight line across her forehead. "You can't help how he feels. That's not your problem."

"As long as *he* understands that." I remembered the way he had glared at me when he left the ranch in the police cruiser. "He thought I should have saved him from the cops somehow."

"Dysfunctional thinking," she said. "There's a lot of that around. Relax. He can't do anything to you here; there are too many people."

I looked at Alphonse and Mary Jane still fondly watching Heather and Sarah, and at the people walking through the big cattle barn. If I had to meet Trevor, I'd rather do it here than in a lonely meadow on the ranch.

"That Alphonse sure makes Heather a good daddy," Paula said in a low voice.

"Yeah, he sure does."

Alphonse is Mary Jane's second husband. Her first husband, Theodore, had been a logger. He was killed by a tree when Heather was two years old. Alphonse and Mary Jane were married when Heather was five, and Alphonse adopted her soon after. "To make sure that lazy brother of Mary Jane's doesn't have any say," Alphonse had told Dad. Today they looked like an advertisement for family solidarity.

Paula spun around. "Look. There's Reena. Let's get her to check our cows." Paula pulled me out of the compound. "Reena," she called. "Hey, wait."

Reena had walked past us, but obligingly turned around. "Hey, yourself."

"Are you here officially? Would you like to check over our cows now?" Paula was like fire, always moving, dancing, lighting up dark places and sparkling with energy.

Reena smiled. "Yes, and sure. Which ones are yours?"

"Here." Paula gestured toward the three heifers. "Edie, Junebug and Evangeline."

Reena followed us into the compound. "Evangeline?" she said, raising an eyebrow and glancing at Paula.

"She's Mike's cow and he likes fancy names. I think it means 'bearer of glad tidings' and Mike hopes she'll bear lots of calves so he can pay for his university."

Reena laughed as she moved between the cows and ran her hands over their shoulders and legs. Each animal had to have a veterinary check. Sick animals couldn't stay in the competition.

"They look superb," she said, when she had finished and marked our names in her notebook. "What are you feeding?"

Paula launched into a detailed account of the new mash she'd been trying. I left them and stepped out of the compound to check on Sarah. She was just walking away with Heather.

"Sarah," I called after her. She turned. "Dad will be here in ten minutes and you haven't given Pansy any water or fixed her stall."

Sarah sighed, but turned back. "Okay. Yeah. All right."

I was relieved that she didn't give me any long excuses or arguments.

"Get the water bucket for me, okay?" she asked.

"No can do," I said.

She shot me a surprised look.

"It's the rules. You know that."

She rolled her eyes in exaggerated resignation. "Oh, yeah. I forgot." She picked up a big rubber bucket and dragged it over to the water tap. She watched the people walking by.

"Sarah," I called, warning her. The bucket was almost overflowing.

"Uh-oh." She jumped back, then darted forward, shutting off the water just in time to avoid a flood.

I looked at the bucket. "You won't be able to carry that."

She tried to lift it and then put it down. "So? Help me."

I shook my head. "Get another bucket and pour half the water into it and make two trips."

"You're a pain, Karen. You could help me."

"I'm not supposed to. I'd get the whole club disqualified from the stall competition." She was supposed to let her hands teach her how to accomplish tasks. Experience is the best teacher. Learn by doing. I knew the theory.

"Well, don't stand there and watch me work. You make me feel like I'm a slave or something."

"Okay. Okay."

I sank onto a chair behind the bales and waited. It was a lot harder to let her do this herself than to do it for her. I wasn't sure I could ever be a mother if it took this much effort. Sarah was struggling back to Pansy's pen with the last bucket of water when someone stopped on the other side of the hay bales.

"Misty Lake 4-H Club," I heard a guy say. "It should be Misty Lake Park. Too many damn cows and not enough dirt bike pits. If we could get rid of the ranches around the lake, we'd have a big park."

I was behind the bales where the newcomers couldn't see me. Other people were walking by. Sarah and I should be safe enough. Maybe the dirt bikers would just keep on walking.

Sarah was on her knees now, picking up the hay that had fallen around Pansy's pen. She wasn't paying any attention to the group at the entrance to the compound. I'd stay quiet; she'd ignore them, and they'd move on.

"Hey, Trev, maybe we should take out a couple of cows now. We could slip in there and cut a few throats."

Trev. Trevor Foster. Just my luck. They'd better not lay a hand on Edie.

"Four steps in, a slash and four steps out."

"Let's try it."

"There's somebody in there."

"It's just a kid."

Sarah looked up at that. Oh-oh. She wouldn't like being called *just* a kid.

"What do you want, big mouth?" No surprise. Sarah always met trouble straight on.

"What's it to you, little turd?"

Sarah jumped to her feet. "You need your mouth washed out."

"Hey," Trevor said. "You're pretty mouthy for a little kid." He walked into the compound, past the hay bales and stopped in front of Sarah. He loomed over her. She stood her ground, a tiny, defiant ant against a threatening giant.

Rage such as I'd never felt before rushed up my body. Hot, seething and uncontrollable like a roaring tide of heat.

"Get away from my sister!" I was standing in front of Trevor with a pitchfork in my hand before I knew I had moved. "Back off!" My voice was loud, strong and full of anger. I raised the pitchfork and leaned toward him. He was not getting near Sarah. "Get out of here!"

There were two guys behind Trevor: Orlan Black and Ron something. Orlan worked at the feed store; I'd seen Ron a couple of times. Sarah said nothing.

Orlan laughed. "Don't let her beat you up, Trev."

Trevor glanced behind and then turned back to me. He raised his hands in mock surrender.

"Pretty tough, aren't you, Karen? Fifty pounds lighter than me and no muscle. I can take that away from you and stick it right through you."

"That's what we should do," Ron said. "Make a broad-on-a-stick."

"Or put it through her foot," Orlan said. "The original stick-in-the-mud." They laughed again.

Three against one and a half. Not good odds. But they were *not* going to touch Sarah if I had to fight like a cougar.

Sarah screamed from somewhere behind me. "Dad!"

Orlan fell back and Ron crumpled to the ground behind Trevor. Dad's hand pressed hard on Trevor's shoulder.

"What's going on?" His deep voice seemed to roll over us.

Trevor froze. I lowered the pitchfork. Sarah grabbed my waist and tucked her head under my arm.

"They threatened Sarah," I said. My hands were shaking and I dropped the pitchfork. Why had I grabbed it? Why hadn't I tried a karate move? I shook my head. What good was all that karate when I never even thought of using it? Stupid, Karen. Really stupid.

"You can't do that." Dad held Trevor so tightly with one hand that Trevor, when he tried to shrug away, couldn't move.

"Let go of me!" Trevor protested.

Dad propelled Trevor around and pointed to his two friends, out cold on the ground. "Don't try it."

Trevor stared. Orlan blinked and raised his head. "What happened, man?"

Alphonse, who had come from nowhere, reached out and gripped Orlan's shoulder. "It'll happen again, kid, if you try to get up. Turn over and put your hands on the back of your head."

"Says who? You a cop?" Orlan struggled for a moment.

"No, but I can put you back to sleep until a cop gets here, or you can turn over right now." Alphonse smiled, but no one was stupid enough to think that he didn't mean it. Orlan stopped moving, stared at him, then turned over.

Ron woke and looked at Orlan. He turned over without being asked and put his hands on the back of his head.

Constable Fraser moved quickly through the crowd that had collected. "Morning, Dan, Alphonse, Mary Jane. What's going on?"

Trevor's voice was high and belligerent. "I was just minding my own business. . . . "

Alphonse interrupted. "It was like this, Will." Will turned

to look at Alphonse, and Dad clipped Trevor behind the ear. Trevor dropped like a sack of feed.

Alphonse was still talking. "They've been cruising around all morning bothering the kids and making comments. I guess they just got a little too aggressive here."

Will turned back to see Dad picking up Trevor and slinging him over his shoulder.

"Guess the kid fainted. Where do you want him?"

Will glanced quickly at Dad and examined Trevor. "I'd better take him in. I'll stop at the clinic and have him checked."

"He should come to in a few seconds. I'll escort him to your car for you." He grinned at Will over Trevor's back. "I don't mind carrying him. If he comes to, he might like to see a familiar face."

"You can stand up now," Alphonse said to his captive.

"Come on, kid," Will said to the silent Ron.

I watched them herd Orlan and Ron and carry Trevor down the alleyway toward the outside door. Alphonse got in behind Dad and took some of Trevor's weight. People parted like grain before the wind, giving trouble lots of room.

Mary Jane picked up the pitchfork and leaned it against the hay bales. Sarah still clung to my side, her hands anchored on my belt. I kept my arm around her.

"So," Mary Jane said. "That was your friend, Trevor."

"Mary Jane?" I said. I wasn't sure what I was asking her for, but I wanted something. She opened her arms and I dove into them, bringing Sarah with me. She hugged us both. Heather slipped in with us and Mary Jane rocked us all.

"You were one brave warrior," she murmured to me. "You can protect my daughter any time. Hey, your mom would be proud."

I sniffed. I was *not* going to cry, I told myself fiercely, but tears spilled down my cheeks.

"You're all right," she crooned. I blinked a few times,

took a deep breath and hugged her harder. She patted my back.

"I think we all need a hot dog. As soon as Alphonse gets back from guard duty, we'll go and get some."

Sarah and Heather stood back. "I don't want mustard on mine," Sarah said, recovering quickly.

"And Heather doesn't want ketchup." Mary Jane finished the litany for her. "Gotcha."

The people who had gathered moved on. Dad and Alphonse walked toward us, talking quietly. Paula and Mike rushed up. Word of the confrontation probably spread in seconds. Paula hugged me, then stood beside me and held my hand with both of hers.

"Are you okay?"

"Yeah. I was scared for a few seconds, but I'm okay now." I had been more angry than scared. And I'd been more than angry; I had been in a totally irrational rage for those few seconds. I hadn't known I was capable of so much feeling.

I looked up to see Kevin walk in the compound. Uh-oh. Had he heard what happened, or had he felt my anger and known something was wrong? He said nothing, just stood back and watched while Paula held my hand and Mary Jane, Alphonse and Dad talked around me. I could see his face was pale; then I noticed his hands hanging down at his sides, clenching and unclenching.

"I'm okay," I said, and held his eyes with mine for a moment. I tried to smile. I'm *really* okay, I said in my mind.

He nodded, then walked away.

Chapter 5

Dad had checked to make sure I was unhurt, patted my shoulder and gone off with Alphonse. Mike arrived to look after his calf. Mike always walks as if he were going to run any minute — quickly, smoothly, like an athlete. He's taller than Dad, thin, dark-skinned and with dark straight hair slicked back away from his face. I was glad to see him. Mary Jane repeated her offer of lunch. I thanked her and declined; I was still shaking inside and I couldn't face a hot dog. Nothing keeps Sarah from food.

"Just stay with Mary Jane," I said as I gave her money.

"Give me a break, Karen. I'm not six years old."

Paula grinned at me. She didn't have a younger sister, and enjoyed Sarah. She also went home when she had had enough of her, while I had to stay and endure.

Sarah skipped off with Heather's family. I felt my shoulders relax. Great. No Sarah. No problems. Time off. An hour without her would give me a chance to do my own chores.

"I'm going to wash Edie."

Paula looked at her watch. "Might as well get it over with before we have to change into our show ring clothes."

"I don't mind washing Evangeline, but I hate having a bath at the same time," Mike grumbled.

Soaping and rinsing a calf Edie's size meant total involvement. If we didn't get water on us when we doused them, we'd get it later when they leaned their wet hides on us or flicked a tail full of water into our faces. I snapped the lead rope on Edie and led her out of her stall. She followed obediently but awkwardly over the concrete floor, stumbling, a little unsure of herself in this strange world of floors, walls and people.

Paula and Mike led their calves in a parade following me through the activities of the barn. Kids pulled and shoved their calves, sheep and pigs in and out of stalls; judges in the aisles contemplated educational displays; someone instructed the next class over the PA system: "Market hogs, Class 6-D. Centre ring, please. Now." Animals called in frustration and irritation. I smelled wood chips, a combination of dust and pitch. It all seemed so comfortable: animals, people and movement. We headed away from the barn to an outside corral, tied the lead ropes to the log rails and rewarded our animals with pats and crooning words of encouragement.

"There you are, Evie, Evie." Mike scratched Evangeline's head. "You're going to be beautiful. Just wait and see."

"She's a nice calf," Paula said, studying Evangeline's conformation. "A little short in the pins, but otherwise quite nice."

Mike had been smiling at her, but now shoved his Stetson back on his head and narrowed his eyes. "Short in the pins, is it? This coming from the owner of the calf that walks on the back of its feet."

"Children, children," I said. "Wait for the judge to decide. May the better calf win. That, of course, will be Edie."

"Not likely!"

"Fat chance!"

I laughed at them. We had been through four judging competitions this season and knew our calves' strengths and weaknesses. They were all good calves, but judges sometimes preferred one animal over the others. So far Paula was ahead on points, but only just.

We washed them using the water from the standing pipe and shared a wet vacuum to pull off water and dirt.

Edie looked wonderful. Her warm brown coat with

splashes of white glistened in the bright sunshine. I aimed the blow-dryer at the patches of wet around her ears and under her neck until she was clean, dry and beautiful. I used both hands to hold the heavy electric clippers and shaved the broad width of her face. She bent her head obligingly for me as I tried to get the hump on the top free from wisps of hair.

Mike's calf, Evangeline, had a long, bushy tail. From the pin on the top of her hips to the beginning of the long, loose hair, it looked like a normal cow's tail. After that, it was a thick brush, like a fox's tail — wavy, luxurious, even elegant. Mike was proud of that tail. He washed, dried and combed it until it fluffed out in a feathery banner. Any judge would take a second look at the calf, just to make sure that tail was real.

I dug the dirt out of Edie's feet with a hoof pick and then polished her hooves with vaseline. She was patient; we had done this whole routine many times. It was soothing.

A picture of Trevor threatening Sarah suddenly flashed into my mind, and I felt weak for a moment. My hands shook. I lay my head against Edie's side and absorbed some of her warmth and steadiness.

"Great cow," a voice said behind me. I looked over my shoulder. Bryan Tyeson, the banker. I'd never seen him in anything but a suit and tie, but today he was dressed in jeans and a red plaid shirt. They were clean and crisp-pressed; he hadn't done any work in them, but they were still western wear. He smiled at me and said again, "Great cow."

"Uh, thanks." He didn't know a heifer from a cow. A heifer like Edie hadn't had a calf, so she wasn't yet a cow. I didn't suppose he really knew anything about cattle, but I recognized a friendly attitude.

He patted Edie's backside. She shrugged a little, but stayed in place. "Your dad tells me you're a real hard worker. Beauty, brains and guts," he said.

For a moment I hesitated. Was he coming on to me, or just being friendly?

"That's right," I said, "totally wonderful, not that Dad's biased or anything like that."

Tyeson laughed. "He might be just a tad biased."

"Just a tad," I agreed, and smiled at him.

"Are you planning on winning your class?" He looked at Edie.

I shrugged. "Naturally. Edie should win it, but Paula and Mike here might disagree. We are competing against each other today."

Tyeson nodded at the other two and narrowed his eyes, critically examining their calves. "Well. . . . " he said.

We waited.

"I have to tell you . . . that I don't know anything about it."

We all laughed with him then. He turned back to me.

"I'd be interested in knowing your plans for the future. We have some scholarships available at the bank, you know."

"No I didn't know."

"You might want to look into it. See me anytime at the bank. I'd be glad to help you out."

"Sure. Thanks." I nodded.

He slapped Edie on the rump. She thought it was a signal to step aside and did. I suppose he thought of Edie as a sofa, or a wall, something inanimate and not a personality that thought and responded. I leaned on her other side and she moved back. Tyeson turned and walked away.

Paula ducked under Junebug's neck and came up beside me. "Why do I feel as if I need a shower after that guy's been around?"

"Hey! He's nice," I said, surprised.

"Money," Mike said, coming up beside her. "It stinks."

"It only stinks on other people." Paula watched Tyeson disappear into the barn. "On me it's odourless."

"I think he's okay," I said. "Just a little uncomfortable

with us, but trying to get along. You're pretty hard on him, Paula."

"Possibly," she said. I continued to look after him and think about what he had said. Maybe it was his job to see those students who might benefit from his bank. He probably checked my name off a list. Maybe this scholarship was available to the children of his customers. I'd go to the bank and ask.

We were leading the calves through the barn to their stalls when Mike spotted a man waiting by the entrance to our compound. "Uh-oh, Karen. Trouble. That's Andy Foster, Trevor's dad. I've seen him at basketball."

I recognized him. I slowed a little, letting Mike and Paula go before me, and studied him. He was shorter than Trevor, much heavier and bald, but with the same dark eyes.

"Hi, Mr. Foster." Mike nodded as he pulled Evangeline into her place and clipped the stall rope to her halter.

"Morning, Mike. Morning." He nodded to Paula.

"Ms. Stewartson?" He looked at me. I stopped. He had only lived in town for a year, but I knew who he was, a realtor and property developer. He must have asked around to find out who I was.

"Yes?" I held Edie's lead rope and waited. Paula and Mike stood by their calves and watched. I saw a couple of 4-H people in the aisle outside the compound. I wasn't going to be alone with this man.

"I'm Andy Foster. I'd like to talk to you for a few minutes."

I hesitated, then started toward Edie's stall. "Just a moment, please." I clipped the stall rope on Edie and patted her neck.

"Do you want me to come with you?" Paula whispered to me over Edie's neck. I nodded. She joined me as I stepped out and walked toward Mr. Foster. Mike moved in behind us.

"I just wanted to talk to Ms. Stewartson." Mr. Foster smiled apologetically at Mike.

I answered. "I'd feel better with my friends around."

Mr. Foster's face turned red. I didn't know if he was angry or embarrassed. He nodded stiffly. "All right. I don't suppose I can blame you. I just wanted you to know that I heard that Trevor had been annoying you."

Annoying me wasn't the way I would have described it. Terrifying me. Scaring me spitless. Intimidating me. I had other words that fit better, but I nodded.

He ran his hand through his hair; the diamonds on his ring finger winked in the light. "I want you to know that, although I realize it may have been only a minor problem . . . that you have my assurance it won't happen again."

I stared at him. What was this? Was this "apology" supposed to make Trevor look better to the police? Mr. Foster was telling me that he was sorry for a minor incident? That I should just forget it? Did he think he could go behind Trevor shovelling problems out of the way, cleaning up after him as if Trevor were a maverick colt? I knew what that made me feel like. No one treated me like that.

"Minor problem!" I stepped closer. "What's a major problem to you then?" I could feel anger simmering and rising like a tide up my body. I didn't think, just opened my mouth and went with the anger like a surfer on the crest of a wave. "Your son's a bully, Mr. Foster. He threatened me and my little sister. She's ten years old. What will he do next? Look for babies and old ladies?"

Mr. Foster backed up. "That's enough! I didn't come here to be abused by you, young lady. I thought the community would expect an apology from Trevor's family, but I wasn't prepared for. . . . "

"Some apology!" I said. "When I came here today I *wasn't prepared* to be threatened by some loser. Telling me that I suffered a 'minor problem' and that you're sorry for the 'annoyance' isn't good enough. What would you say if he'd actually hit my sister? Or put that pitchfork through foot? 'Sorry? Trevor has a little trouble with his temper?' You've got big problems with Trevor, Mr Foster."

He leaned toward me until his face was only inches from mine. "You are a sharp-tongued little witch. Maybe you contribute to your own problems."

I stood where I was. There were three of us and *this* time I was going to remember my karate. "The next thing I'll hear from you, Mr. Foster, will be that it's *my* fault Trevor can't control himself. Blaming the victim isn't cool today, don't you know? The problem here belongs to Trevor. He's a dangerous guy. And blaming me isn't going to make him less dangerous."

"Look." His face was red again, but this time I was sure it was anger. "I'm trying to say that I'm sorry you were bothered by Trevor and I'll see that you aren't bothered again."

"Sorry, Mr. Foster." Paula spoke firmly. "We don't think you're doing such a good job with Trevor right now. Your guarantees aren't worth much."

Mr. Foster looked at Mike with a we're-guys-together kind of look. "Can't you talk some sense into these girls?"

Mike wasn't having any of it. "Get real, man. I'm on their side. They don't take shit from no one. Why should they?"

Mr. Foster's eyebrows rose. He acted as if he'd stopped to pet a kitten and been bitten by a lynx. Then he turned quickly and strode from the compound, past the people waiting at the entrance and down the aisle.

Mr. Jennings stayed in position at the entrance of the compound. Mike's mom turned away and Paula's mom went back to the educational display she had been judging. I knew they had been watching, letting me handle the problem, but there if I needed them. Mr. Jennings smiled, lifted a hand and turned back toward the refreshment stand.

"I feel kind of sorry for the poor guy," Paula said as she put her lead rope in with Mike's and mine in the tack box.

"Why?"

"Imagine having Trevor for a son. It would be li'

housing an undisciplined pit bull. What a trip."

"Yeah." I was thoughtful. It would be hard to go around apologizing for your kid. I wondered what Mom would say about that. Actually, I knew what Mom would say and do. To start with, she wouldn't go around apologizing for me; she'd tell me to apologize for myself, and she'd stand behind me to make me do it, too. I shook my head. I felt a little sorry for Mr. Foster myself, but I still didn't want anything to do with him.

"Karen!" Sarah dashed into the compound. "You've got to help me. My class is on in two minutes."

I ran my eyes over her quickly. "Tuck in your shirt. Where's your number?"

She held it out to me.

"Turn around. I'll pin it on you. Do you have Pansy's lead rope?"

She held up her other arm.

"Great, Sarah. You're organized."

"Mary Jane helped me."

I grinned. "Honest, too. What do you have to remember about the class?"

"Don't stand between Pansy and the judge no matter where the judge is. Move so the judge gets a good look at her." She recited her lessons to me. "Hey, Karen. I'm in trouble. I didn't spend enough time with Pansy. She isn't very good in the ring. She jumps around and doesn't want to stand still."

Now Sarah worried. She should have worried about this months ago. I knew she hadn't spent much time with Pansy, but Mom said a poor showing would teach Sarah to be more conscientious in the future, so no one had nagged her very much about training.

"st try to present her to the judge as well as you can,"

nsy jumps grab her — "

e neck. I know."

I watched from the stands as Sarah joined her class of six juniors with breeding ewes. They paraded around in a circle, staying on the outside of their lambs so the judge in the centre could see the way the lambs moved. The competition would be close, and it didn't look good for Sarah. Pansy jumped if another animal coughed, and skittered away from the judge whenever she came close.

Sarah was doing well, holding Pansy and patiently placing her feet back in position every time she jumped, which was often, but that wouldn't have been necessary if Sarah had gone out every day after school and worked with Pansy. Sarah's ears were red, which is a good sign that she's only barely holding onto her temper. If Sarah lost her temper, things would only get worse out there. I bit my fingernail and hoped she could just get through this. The judge picked out four ewes to place. Sarah's was one of the four, so she had to move inside the circle. Pansy didn't want to move, and jumped and twitched trying to get away. Sarah hung onto her, determined to get her into that placing line.

She managed it, too, and for a fourth-place ribbon. Pansy even shied away from the ribbon as Sarah took it. Sarah held her firmly under the chin, forcing her back into position. At least Pansy didn't break free. A sheep chase through the barns would have been wild.

I had stood to leave the stands and join Sarah when the judge took the mike. "Ladies and gentlemen, parents and 4-Hers. I have been asked to choose a candidate for best presenter here today. This is the last competition for this event, so I am able to announce the winner of the junior presenter class. For parents and older members, I might remind you that this used to be called the showmanship class. I am pleased to announce that #317 is the winner, Sarah Stewartson."

I stood immobile. This couldn't be true! Sarah? Winning a presenter class? Sarah? Who had spent so little time on her sheep that it couldn't behave?

The judge walked over and gave Sarah a white rosette and continued. "Sarah has done an excellent job with a very nervous ewe. Congratulations!"

Sarah smiled as if she'd earned that ribbon! I looked over at Mary Jane. She rolled her eyes.

"It's not fair," I said. I knew that Heather had spent hours practising with her ewe. Mary Jane nodded.

"It will teach the others how to tolerate some injustice all right."

"But what is it going to teach Sarah?"

"Sarah is one of those kids who slips on the cow dung and lands in the butter every time," Mary Jane said. "She'll always do just fine."

I shook my head and headed for the gate and Sarah.

"Hey, what you think?" Sarah said excitedly as I approached her.

Pansy pulled back on her halter and started swinging her head from side to side. I grabbed the rosette Sarah was showing me and reached for the lead rope.

"Let's just get this 'highly nervous' beast into her pen. And good for you, Squirt." I might as well praise her. She did win the ribbon.

Later that afternoon when I was standing in front of the judges giving my demonstration of karate moves, I felt as if I was carrying on a family tradition of hypocrisy. Here I was, telling everyone how to defend themselves, and when I'd had an emergency, karate had flown out of my mind. What good was karate if I didn't use it when I needed it?

I went through my memorized instructions, Paula obligingly falling with my fake lunges. It was a simple demonstration. My 4-H leader had told me that I should try to convey only three ideas in a four-minute talk, so that's I did.

H members demonstrated different topics: making omelets, creating a clay pot and making a kite. I knew the kite-making one wasn't going to win, because the demonstrators tried to teach us about sixteen things in four minutes, and we were pretty confused by the time they finished. Sarah watched my demonstration, rolling her eyes and making faces at me during the whole thing, but she cheered when they announced I was the winner. I felt like a fraud taking the rosette, but I'd have felt even more foolish trying to decline it on the grounds that I was a hypocrite who didn't deserve it, so I took it, smiled and said thanks.

Bryan Tyeson was one of the people who congratulated me. The bank had supported the 4-H sale, and the supporters usually attended some of the events.

"Very nicely done," he said to me. His blue eyes twinkled. "I'll be sure not to meet you in any dark alleys." I smiled and felt even more of a fraud. He was safe from me in broad daylight or dark alleys. I didn't really know how to use karate.

"Thanks, Paula," I said as we changed in the bathroom. We had our dress clothes for the dance with us because we didn't have time to go home. "I wasn't nervous up there at all because you were with me."

She hugged me. "Any time, old girl. Think they'll let me come with you to the PNE?"

"What?"

She grinned. "Didn't you know? You just won a spot in the Pacific National Exhibition in Vancouver next week. You'll have to go and compete."

"Oh, no! I've got too much to do."

"Sarah also won a spot. Didn't you realize that?"

"You're kidding!"

"No. All winners on the livestock presentations, junior and senior, judging and demonstrations get a trip to compete in Vancouver. That's you and Sarah and, if I win the judging, me. And . . . ." She stopped for a second to calculate. "Two others."

I sat down on the counter. "I'd forgotten about that. Next week! The PNE is next week?"

"Yep. We leave Tuesday and get back on Friday. My mom's a chaperon, that's why I know about it. And, of course, I expect to win the judging, so I needed to know when I'd be away."

She sounded smug, but I knew she had a good chance at the judging competition; her marks had been high all year. I thought about four days in Vancouver at the fair.

"It'd be a blast with you, Paula. We could hit the band concerts and . . . but I'd have to look after Sarah."

"The chaperon will look after Sarah."

"It takes an army to look after Sarah."

"She's something, all right."

"What are you wearing tonight?" I looked at the clothes in Paula's small suitcase. "The purple mini?"

Dad had promised us hamburgers in half an hour, before he took us to the dance upstairs in the livestock meeting room.

"Yeah, my purple mini, long shirt and these earrings." She pushed the posts through her ears and let the purple and silver beads dangle down. "Mary Jane made them for me."

I admired them. "They're great."

I shook out my new black jeans and my bright turquoise shirt and placed them on the counter, then folded my *gi* and put it into my suitcase.

"Nice," Paula said, looking at my shirt. "What earrings are you wearing?" I showed her. Some girls at my school criticize each other's clothes and each other's figures and hair, but Paula was never like that. If she didn't like something I wore, she just didn't say anything about it. I pulled on my new black western boots and admired the shine on the leather.

going to meet me at the concession stand," "and we're going to the dance from there. Do you want to come with us?"

I shook my head. "Dad said he'd spring for the hamburgers, and I told Kevin I'd meet him at the dance. Maybe I'll meet him at the concession stand. I'm not sure."

"You and Kevin, hmm?"

I caught her eyes in the mirror. "Funny, isn't it?" I said.
"Why?"

"After knowing him all these years and then. . . . "

"And then you suddenly notice he's a man?"

"Something like that."

"Funny and confusing?"

I felt a red flush on my face. I guess I'd noticed all right, but I hadn't admitted it. I then looked back at her sharply. "So? Are you noticing Mike?"

She shrugged, then carefully sprayed purple dye into her bangs and combed it through. The dye screamed a magenta statement against the dark brown of the rest of her hair. "I've noticed Mike before. He's just beginning to notice me."

"So much for 'not being serious.'"

"We'll see. I don't want to ruin a good friendship."

"That's the problem, isn't it? And then both Mike and Kev leave for college in three weeks." I combed out my braid and left my hair loose. It sprang away from my head in the waves the braid had forced into it. A little hair spray made it shiny. I scrunched the ends and then shook my head so that it fell evenly around my shoulders.

"Looking good, Karen," Paula said as we picked up our suitcases and headed for the door.

"As good as it gets," I said. "The purple you're wearing is good with the earrings. What's with the hair?"

"It gives Mike something to notice and to worry about. He's never sure if I'm truly off the wall or only pretending to be."

Mike noticed, all right. He dropped his hamburge when he saw her.

Chapter 6

The meeting room was decorated with balloons and a big, green 4-H sign. Someone had connected a five-disk CD player and stacked CDs ready for the dance. Conversation flittered around us as we walked toward the refreshment tables. Everyone brought baked goods or packages of chips and Cheezies and deposited them on three long tables. I'd taken some of Mom's chocolate chip cookies from the freezer — a fact Sarah announced to everyone.

"You don't have to worry," she told Mary Jane in a loud voice. "Karen didn't make them; Mom did. They'll be good."

Mary Jane darted a glance at me, then shook her head at Sarah. "That wasn't kind, little one."

Sarah looked surprised and then thoughtful. "You mean I was putting Karen down?"

Mary Jane nodded.

"Oh." Sarah turned to me and tilted her head to one side. For a brief moment she considered an apology, then gave up the idea and dashed away after one of her friends. I let out a long sigh and watched her run away.

"Take the night off, Karen," Mary Jane said.

I nodded. "Dad will look after her." I was going to forget her, relax and enjoy myself tonight.

The first person I saw when I turned away from Sarah was Andy Foster standing on the other side of the room. heart jumped before I told myself not to be ridiculous. angry earlier, but he wasn't looking at me now. g to Bryan Tyeson, leaning toward him, ges- his coffee cup, explaining something. Mr.

Foster wasn't going to yell at me here at the dance with all the parents around. Just to be sure, though, I was going to stay well away from him.

"Come on, Karen." Kevin grabbed my hand. "They're playing 'Cadillac Ranch.' Let's party!" I waved to Paula. She grinned and turned to Mike as he pulled her into the dance.

It was a line dance and I loved them. Everyone at our school took dancing: line dancing, waltzing and jiving. Most kids could really dance. The line dances were the best. Everyone — teens, parents and little kids — did the same steps at the same time, changing steps when the music changed in a sort of a musical team sport. Boots banged on the wooden floor, hands clapped in unison, bodies swayed in synchronous movement. The music sang in my bones and drummed through my head like a heartbeat.

Kevin and I danced four line dances and then a waltz. Someone turned the lights down for the slow music. I drifted around the dance floor, my arms around Kevin's waist, tired from the strenuous dances and feeling a little dreamy in the semi-darkness.

That night when I'd dressed for the dance, I had thought of Kevin and hoped he would like my new turquoise shirt and my silver earrings. The earrings even tinkled a little when I moved. He must have noticed them. I thought he might have said something about how I looked, but all he said was, "You smell so good." I suppose that is better than smelling bad, but it didn't seem to be much of a compliment. Was smelling good important? I don't think I know *anything* about looking seductive or attractive.

About ten o'clock I danced past Sarah, who was stretched out on two chairs, sound asleep. Dad sat beside her, talking to two ranchers from the Black Creek area. When the dance ended, I wandered over to a spot near Dad, dropped down onto a chair and watched Sarah sleep, her head pillowed on her arms, eyes closed and mouth slightly open. The freckles across her nose seemed to stand out against her pale skin. I could have counted them. "Kind of cute, isn't she, Dad?"

"Yeah, she is."

"She whirls around like a wind-up toy and then she crashes."

Dad nodded and gently moved Sarah's hair off her forehead. "She has a lot of energy and vitality," he said. "She reminds me of a weed, maybe a dandelion — always around, hard to ignore, but full of sunshine and bright lights."

I thought about dandelions for a moment. Sarah *was* like that.

"What am I then, Dad?"

He looked at me thoughtfully and turned away a little, so the men couldn't hear him. "You're a weed too, Karen. Tenacious, determined to survive. But you're more like a columbine, full of the beauty of the woods, moving in winds no one else can feel."

I stared at him for a moment. It amazed me that Dad could see me that way, and it scared me a little. I didn't want to "move in winds no one else could feel." That was too weird. I wanted to be ordinary like clover — useful to the land, common and close to the ground where the winds wouldn't affect me. I glanced back at Dad. "What about Mom?"

He lifted his head and looked away for a moment. "Your mother's a rose, a red, red rose. Beautiful, magical and necessary for the survival of the soul." He smiled then, and turned back to his conversation with the men.

My dad is a poet, a musician and different from anyone else I know. But then, maybe I just didn't know other people well. Mary Jane seemed to think that I missed a lot.

ed back at Sarah and thought how sweet she
hen she was sleeping, as if she was one of those

model kids on television, all smiles and shy glances. What an illusion! Sarah didn't do shy.

I heard the men talking, but I didn't join the conversation. They were talking about land. They always talked about land: how to hay it, how to fertilize it, how to irrigate it. This time they were talking about how to sell it.

"I may have to sell," one of the men said. "Had such a run of bad luck lately, calves dying, hay not as good as I wanted, that I've been thinking of getting out altogether. I have my welding ticket, so I can move to town and set up a shop there. Kind of hate to do it, but I've got a good offer from the Shandon Development Company for the land. Foster thinks they can put a few recreational lots on my place."

"Away from the lake the way you are, John?" Dad asked. "Why would your land make good recreational property?"

"Apparently they're buying up property for cross-country skiing and just get-away-from-it-all vacation homes. Almost any land in the country is saleable right now. What about you, Dan?"

Dad took his time, but answered quietly. "I'm not selling. I don't want to do anything but ranch. If I sell the ranch I'd only have money, and money wouldn't suit me. If I had money, I'd have to play golf. It'd make me crazy in no time."

The men laughed. Dad continued.

"Nope, I hope to hold on. I guess that's all I can say. I hope to hold on."

I looked away, pretending not to hear their conversation, but glad Dad had said that about keeping the ranch. I couldn't imagine not walking out to the far meadow in the summer or skating on the lake in the winter. I didn't *want* to imagine coming home from university to a house in town. What would happen to Edie and my other cows if Dad sold the ranch? How could Mom and Dad keep Sarah busy on a town lot?

Mr. Tyeson came up then and asked me to dance. We did a fast two-step. He led smoothly and was easy to follow.

"Congratulations, Karen," Tyeson said. He twirled me and then continued. "Karate's a good idea. You never know when a girl will need to defend herself."

I said politely, "Thanks, Mr. Tyeson."

"Bryan," he said, and squeezed my shoulder.

I inched back. "My dad wouldn't like me to call you that, Mr. Tyeson."

"Oh, I see," he said. "No problem. I guess you'll be going to the PNE with your win in the demonstration?" He indicated a turn with the pressure of his hand. I twirled, faced him again and nodded.

"Is your dad going down with you?"

I shook my head. "No, he has a lot to do on the ranch. We'll have chaperons, though."

"I'm sure you'll enjoy a few days away from home." He smiled down at me, his eyes twinkling as if he knew a joke that I didn't. "You seem to be a young woman who knows her own mind. I'm sure you'll manage to have a good time."

"Yes, I don't get to Vancouver very often."

I hated this kind of conversation. Was he telling me that he thought I was a good-time party girl? I wished he would just say what he meant.

"I understand you had a problem with Trevor Foster today?" He nodded at a couple passing near us.

Uh-oh. Given a choice, I'd have taken polite word games over talk about Trevor.

"He was a problem, yes." It seemed to me that Mr. Foster, a real estate salesman, and Mr. Tyeson, a banker, knew each other pretty well. They'd been talking together earlier. Had they been talking about me? Had Mr. Foster told Tyeson the things I'd said? I remembered some of them: Trevor's a bully; he's dangerous. Was Tyeson going to criticize me? My shoulders tensed and I felt my body stiffen.

"The way I heard it, he attacked your sister and you sent him packing. Good for you! Karate?"

"Pitchfork."

He laughed.

I relaxed a little. He hadn't heard the story that way from Andy Foster.

"You're quite a woman." He squeezed my shoulders.

Now I was definitely uneasy. I inched away.

"That Foster kid is a little stupid."

"Trevor? I don't think he's stupid."

"Self-centred might be a better word," he said.

Nasty would be more accurate, I thought, and dangerous. The dance ended. Mr. Tyeson thanked me. I nodded and left him.

He made me uncomfortable. He was friendly, but maybe too friendly. Was he coming on to me? He was old enough to be my father. Did that matter? All the guidance posters at school said Trust Your Instincts, but I didn't know if I was reacting with instincts or ignorance.

"Last waltz." Kevin came up behind me, put his hand on my shoulder and turned me into his arms.

They always dim the lights and play romantic music for the last waltz at 4-H dances. I think they do it so married couples can feel nostalgic and loving toward each other before they go home. The rest of us are always aware that our parents are not far away; we just waltz.

"Ready to go?" Kevin asked.

"Sure, I'll tell Dad."

"I told him," Kevin said.

I shot a look at him. "I'll tell him myself."

"Okay, okay."

Dad just nodded when I said I was going home with Kevin and gathered Sarah up in his arms.

Kevin took my hand. We stepped outside and walked toward his truck in the parking lot, calling good night to people who were heading for their vehicles.

We talked about the dance and the 4-H show until Kevin pulled off the direct route home and into the mill road trail.

"Where are you going?" I knew where he was going. Off the road into isolation.

"I want to talk to you without your dad or Sarah interfering."

"Talk?" I could handle talk. I wasn't afraid of Kevin, but parking in an isolated spot in the woods might stir up more intimacy than I wanted. I needed to know what he had in mind.

"Kevin?"

"Relax. I promise you, I'm not going to do anything you don't want. I want to talk about our psychic sense."

"Oh?" I did relax then. He was right. We needed to talk about the feelings we were sending to each other. I didn't want to run to him every time he felt upset, and he didn't need to pop up beside me every time I lost my temper.

He pulled off at the mill site and parked on the sawdust. We could see the lake and the lights of his house and mine. He shut off the motor. There was silence, and then slowly small sounds seemed to get louder. A mosquito whined near my ear. A branch snapped in the woods. An owl's soft call drifted out onto the night air. It was incredibly beautiful.

"So," Kevin said, stretching his legs and leaning back. His hand was draped along the top of the seat. "Are you going to let me in?"

I turned to face him. "Into my mind, you mean?"

"Yeah. When you feel something real strong, are you going to call for me?" He turned now so that his back was against the door, leaving space between us, but it felt intimate, dark and isolated. It was as if we were the only two people in the world right now and as if only total honesty was possible.

"You come in," I said, "whether or not I want you. You felt me this afternoon. I didn't even think of you, but you knew, didn't you?"

"I knew something was wrong. I got a strong wave of fear and anger."

I nodded. "Sometimes it's like that."

"You can stop it if you decide you don't want me there. You've kept me out for years." He shifted back so that he was looking out the front window, both hands on the steering wheel.

I shrugged uncomfortably and stared out the window as well. "It wasn't just me. You blocked me out too."

"I know. I was growing up, I guess. I wanted privacy. But now, I want to be back in touch with you." He turned, closer now. "I want that passage to your mind." His hand drifted down to my shoulder. I felt his fingers playing with the ends of my hair.

"Why?" I lifted my chin and stared straight at him.

"Look." He dropped his hand in exasperation and matched my straight look. "Don't get too analytical about this. Whatever happens between us, I want you on my wavelength. It's special. It's never happened with anyone else and it's not going to happen with anyone else. At least not for me." He tilted his head back and waited.

"No," I said slowly. "It's never happened with anyone else. I don't know why it's you."

He started to speak and then stopped, waited a moment and said. "So, will you let me in?"

I stared at the lake, thinking about the special communication we had. Was it a good thing? Would it hurt me? How could it hurt me?

"Promise, Kay?" He only called me that when something really mattered. If I promised to let him into my mind, I was on my honour to do that. The flip side was *not* to let him in. Not to have that special communication. Not to have him on my side.

"Okay," I said.

He let out a long sigh. "Great."

I wasn't quite sure what I had just committed myself to. Then he lifted his hand and ran his finger down my cheek. "So, do you think we could move this relationship along a little further in other ways?"

Romance? Commitment? He was talking about intimacy. I'd just agreed to mental intimacy, and now he wanted physical intimacy?

"Hey." I sat up quickly. "Now that's stupid."

"For God's sake, what now!" He sounded angry. Then he took a deep breath and asked more calmly, "Why is it stupid?"

I spoke rapidly. "Look, Kev. It's one thing to let the psychic waves flow; it's another to start a romance. You're going away to school. I've got one more year of high school, then eight years of university. It would be just stupid to 'move this relationship along.'"

"Are you finished?" I could feel his arms stiffen as I talked, and I heard the annoyance in his voice. The moonlight put his eyes in shadows, but his shoulders suddenly seemed huge and rigid.

He leaned closer. "You are so reasonable that you lose yourself in all those picky reasons! Are you planning on living in a glass cage for nine years without ever being involved with anyone?"

When he said that, I felt foolish. "Uh, probably not."

"Listen," he said. "I've got five years to a business degree before I come back to the ranch. We both have a life to plan, things to do. 'Getting involved' is not an either-or situation — either I get a business degree *or* I get involved with you." His voice rose and he spoke emphatically. "Getting a vet degree is not the *only* thing you can do in nine years. We can do both: get our degrees and get to know one another. Unless you are trying to tell me that you can't stand me and you don't want anything to do with me. If you are, tell me straight and get it over with."

I thought for a moment. "I'm not trying to tell you that."

"Good."

"But Kev, you're going to be gone. What kind of a relationship can we have?"

"Well, for one thing, birth control shouldn't be a problem — if I'm in Vancouver and you're here."

I laughed. "Kevin, really."

He leaned forward and played with the ends of my hair again. "I don't know, Karen, we could just see where it goes. I'm not asking for forever, and I'm not asking for your body. I'm just asking for a little involvement. Right now a good-night kiss would be great."

"Just a good-night kiss?" I started to smile as I looked up at him. I reached out and trailed my fingers along his chin. It was rough and prickly. "I don't know, Kevin. The last time we kissed it was a big flop."

He leaned forward. "Give me a break. I was twelve." His eyes lit with humour. He had always been able to smile with his eyes.

"Okay," I whispered.

I expected him to lean forward and kiss me, but he reached over and snapped my seat belt open and then his own, put his hands on my hips and pulled me closer.

I tensed a little.

He feathered a kiss along my lower lip with soft pressure, almost as if he was teasing me. I relaxed and leaned into him. Then he pulled me tight, slanted his mouth and deepened the kiss. Heat shot through me and I felt as if all my bones had disappeared. We seemed to meld together like that for a long time. I kissed him back, enjoying the feel and smell of him. He pulled back and butted his forehead on mine.

"You are really something."

I sucked in oxygen and tried to steady my voice. "Not fair, Kev."

"What's not fair?"

"You've been practising since sixth grade."

He grinned.

Chapter 7

Dad was on the phone when I walked into the kitchen. One o'clock at our house was two in Edmonton, so Mom must have been sitting in Grandma's kitchen watching the city lights and feeling a little lonely for us. Dad smiled and waved at me, indicating that I should take the receiver. He put the phone to one side and spoke to me as I walked across the floor. "You okay?"

I rolled my eyes at him. What did he think happened between the dance and home? "Of course, I'm okay. Kevin's a nice guy, Dad."

"No guy's a nice guy," he muttered.

"Mom!" I protested as I put the receiver to my ear.

"Have patience, Karen," she said. "He'll get used to it."

"I'm almost seventeen. You'd think I was. . . . "

"I know," she said, "but you haven't dated much and he's naturally protective. You can't have a loving, caring dad without getting the flip side once in a while."

"You mean nosy, overbearing and irritating?"

"Yes, that's what I mean." Then we laughed. "Tell me about the show."

So I told her about the demonstration competition and about my win and Sarah's win. "It was really unfair, Mom. Heather practised much more than Sarah and then Sarah won!"

"Totally unfair," Mom agreed. "How did Heather feel?"

"I don't know." I hadn't thought to ask her.

"Maybe you could suggest to Sarah that she tell Heather how much she wishes Heather were going to the

PNE with her." I listened carefully. Mom was asking me to guide Sarah, make her think. I wasn't sure I could do it.

"Not how much she wishes Heather had won?"

"Let's not expect too much of Sarah; she doesn't wish Heather had won. Sarah likes winning." To be honest, I liked winning too.

I said I'd do my best and asked her about Grandma. I wanted to talk about Kevin and ask Mom if what I felt for him was real or even important, but I wasn't going to talk about Kevin with Dad standing right there.

Then Mom said, "How was your date with Kevin?"

"It was fine," I said, and waited.

There was a short silence, then Mom said, "Do you need anything, Karen? I hate being so far away right now, but your grandmother isn't adjusting to her dependent life very well and I don't think I can leave her yet."

"I'm fine, Mom."

"Do you need any medical advice?"

I felt a flush of heat travel over my face. "No! Mom, really! I just had one date. Don't get so serious on me." What did she think I was doing?

"Okay, honey. You know yourself best. Just remember to do only what *you* want to do."

"Okay, okay." I didn't want a lecture on sexual behaviour right now. I changed the subject quickly. "Hey, Mom. Don't stay away too long. I can't keep up this pace: dishes, cooking, Sarah, 4-H, Sarah, mail, Sarah."

She laughed and I handed the phone back to Dad.

I was embarrassed by Mom's questions. Kevin and I weren't a big item. We just had one date. One kiss. It wasn't a relationship. It might never be a relationship. I wished Mom and Dad wouldn't force me into thinking about it. There was nothing to think about. I left them talking and went to bed. It hit me just before I dropped into sleep that maybe I *should* think about it.

In the morning Dad was up, whistling and making pancakes in the kitchen before I had had enough sleep. I heard Sarah in the shower and waited until the water stopped running before I finally pushed myself out of bed and took my own quick shower.

"Are four pancakes okay?" Dad asked as I wandered into the kitchen.

"Four are great." I yawned and poured myself some orange juice. "What did Mom say last night about coming home?"

Dad stopped whistling and glanced at me. "She said Grandma is going to need her for at least another week."

I stared at my orange juice. "Bummer."

"Yeah. That's how I feel too."

I turned my glass around and around in my hands. Dad walked past me to get milk from the fridge and patted my head. I smiled, but kept my eyes on my glass.

"She'll be back," he said.

"I know."

"She said she'd call the post office and have them look after the mail delivery for the Tuesday to Friday runs while you're away. She was really proud of you guys for doing so well in the 4-H show."

I looked up quickly. "I forgot about the mail."

Dad added milk, stirred and poured pancakes into fat, round circles on the griddle. "You'll be here on Monday, won't you?"

I nodded. "We leave for Vancouver Tuesday morning, back Thursday night."

Dad set the bowl of batter on the counter and reached for the spatula. He talked to me while he watched the pancakes cook. "She thought you'd be too tired on Friday to do the run, so she arranged for a temporary replacement."

Mom in Edmonton had thought of all that. I didn't know why, but I felt like crying. "I just forgot about the mail."

Dad tested a pancake by lifting an edge. He peered

under it before he let it drop back. "It's all okay."

"I should have remembered it, though."

"You have a lot to think about now."

I looked at him sharply, but he was flipping pancakes and didn't notice. How did he know what I was thinking?

"What with all the chores," he continued as he set four pancakes on a plate in front of me, "and most of the cooking and everything. It's no wonder you forgot."

I did have too many chores to do. "And then there's the poisonings," I said. "That worries me a lot. Three calves, Dad." The steamy smell of pancakes reminded me I was hungry. I reached for the syrup.

"Actually," Dad said as he brought his pancakes to the table and sat down, "it's four."

"Which one?" I paused with the fork halfway to my mouth.

"Number 49's calf. The calf with the odd ear."

I remembered it: tall in the shoulders, a broad head. "That was a good calf."

Dad nodded. "Yeah. They were all good calves, and now they are all dead calves."

I stared at him. He stiffened, then swore under his breath, shot to his feet and started pacing up and down the kitchen.

"Senseless. Stupid. Criminal," he muttered. "Good calves all of them."

"That's right," I said, watching him.

He strode out onto the porch. I saw him through the window, standing at the edge of the deck, banging his fist on the railing. Then he turned and walked back into the kitchen. He pushed his hair back, smiled at me and sat down to his breakfast.

"Feel better?" I asked.

"Much. I'm going to start patrolling once in the night. That's about all I can manage and still work the next day.

Maybe I can catch whoever's doing this." He suddenly gave serious, enthusiastic attention to his pancakes.

I pushed a piece of pancake around in the syrup, thinking about the poisonings. "It's so sick."

Dad nodded. We ate silently for a few minutes.

"Dad, do you think these poisonings might have something to do with the developers who want the ranch?"

Dad raised an eyebrow. "How so?"

"I mean, Andy Foster is trying to get ranchers from around here to sell their land. Maybe he's putting together a big land tract and needs more land to make a . . . a . . . financially worthwhile development."

Dad sipped his coffee and thought about it. "That's smart, Karen. Possible, even. But I don't see why he'd have to resort to poisoning our stock. There are ranchers around here who will sell — in time, anyway."

"But we have the lake property, and maybe he doesn't have time. A big development company might be trying to buy up tracts of land all over the country. Maybe he has to have it soon. It would be easy for him to get Trevor and his friends to drop the poison around."

"Hmmm." Dad pushed his empty plate away and leaned his elbows on the table. "Kind of hard to believe that a man would send his son out to do that kind of dirty work."

"He probably thinks that we owe him the land, or we don't deserve to have it. I heard Trevor say something about the land should be a park so dirt bikers could use it. Maybe they feel justified."

Dad rubbed the back of his neck and stared at the wall for a few minutes, then spoke as he thought the idea through. "Andy Foster will only make a commission on his sales. He can't own a development company; there are real estate laws that prevent that. So I don't think it's Andy. Everything he does is easy to trace because real estate laws look after that." He paused for a moment, then shook his head. "It's a good theory, Karen, but it won't fit. It would be too easy to prove he was outside the law. And . . . he's not so stupid he wouldn't see that."

It made so much sense to have Andy Foster behind the poisonings that I didn't want to let the idea go. "If there was a way he could do it and not get caught, I bet he'd do it. What do they say about crime on TV? All you need is no conscience, opportunity and a payoff. Suppose he doesn't have a conscience. Trevor could be his opportunity, and the lake property his payoff."

Dad shook his head. "I don't think so, Karen, but I'll tell Constable Fraser your ideas." At least, Dad had listened to me. I felt better for having told him.

"Fraser invited me to a meeting tomorrow," he continued. "I guess Trevor's having a hearing in Family Court this week. He's never been in trouble before, so they want to keep him out of the justice system. See what the community can come up with to deal with him."

"You mean community service?" We had a system here that allowed first-time juvenile offenders to work off their problems without actually getting a criminal record. Second offenders landed in the criminal justice system with fines, probation or even jail terms.

Dad nodded. "He wants me to appear to describe what Trevor actually did."

"I hope you can get it through Trevor's egotistical skull that the universe doesn't revolve around him."

Dad got up to get more coffee. "I'll try."

Sarah bounced in just then, looking for her breakfast. "So how was your big date?" she said, and slipped onto a chair. I groaned. There was a good chance I'd never date again if my family didn't stop hassling me.

"Boring," I lied.

"No, really?" Sarah stopped pouring orange juice for a moment and looked at me. "Why? Didn't you kiss and do all that stuff they do on TV?"

I knew I blushed. I could feel the heat on my face. "Get real, Sarah."

"Heather says that's what her cousins do. She says you and Kevin probably do that too."

"Heather doesn't know anything," I said.

"Thank goodness," Dad murmured as he set Sarah's pancakes in front of her.

I laughed. "Yeah. Thank goodness."

Sarah lost interest and attacked her pancakes.

We try to make Sunday a lazy day, but we still have chores to do and animals to feed. After an hour, when I had most of my chores finished, Paula called on the phone and arranged to meet me to talk about the night before.

I launched the canoe easily from our shore and paddled down the lake, noticing the clouds bunching up beyond the trees at the Jennings' end. The sky was clear overhead, though, and the air was still. I docked at the landing halfway down the lake opposite Kevin's place just as Paula rode up on her mare. She looped Sheeba's reins around a pole and joined me on a log that jutted out over the water. We sat with our feet hanging down just above the green glass of the lake.

"So," Paula said. "How was the hot date?"

I didn't mind the question from Paula. "Hotter than I expected."

She laughed. "Good old Kevin?"

I nodded. "Good old Kevin. How was Mike?"

"Doing nicely," she said.

I breathed in the pine-scented air, letting the sunshine warm my shoulders and relax my tense muscles. A loon popped up near us, curious about the disturbance in his bay, then dived back down. I could see him darting errati-cally in the clear, green water. Weeds streamed with the current below the surface, their dark green and bright yellow undersides interchanging as they moved like thin dancers to water music. A hummingbird hovered in front of me, attracted momentarily to my bright red T-shirt. Its wings buzzed with frenzied activity as it hung in the air for a second, then darted away.

"Paula?"

"Uh-huh?"

"You went with Allan for three years, grades nine, ten and eleven. What happened?"

"You mean what happened to get us together? What happened to break us up? What kind of relationship did we have?"

"What kind of a relationship?"

"You know what kind it was, Karen. Easy. Nonthreatening. Unexciting. Asexual."

"Why did you go with him?"

She shoved her dark curls away from her face, looked over the bay toward the far shore and stayed very still for a moment. Then she said, "We had decided at the beginning of grade nine that if we stuck together as an item, no one would harass us to be part of a different couple and no one would accuse us of being gay. Remember when that was such a worry in ninth grade?"

I nodded. For some reason, there was a lot of pressure on us in that year to prove we were heterosexual. I didn't know what being *sexual* meant in those days, much less hetero. In those days, I just wanted boys to leave me alone.

"Anyway, we teamed up for parties and movies and stuff and it worked great because we got to socialize and never had to deal with heavy stuff — feelings, sex, demands."

"Didn't you ever kiss him?"

"Sure, I kissed him." She dabbled one pink painted toe in and out of the lake, watching the water move around it. "I know drums are supposed to roll and skies rip apart, but when Allan kissed me, nothing happened. It was more or less just friendly. Easy, actually."

Drums, I thought. I didn't hear drums last night. Cymbals, maybe, and a roaring wind.

"And," she continued, "neither of us met anyone else we really wanted to know better. You know our classes. Who's to know?"

I smiled at her. "Mike?"

"Well, yeah, Mike. He was a year ahead of us and I didn't see him in those days." She leaned over to pick up a handful of pebbles from the bank, and tossed them into the lake one by one. "In those days, I had a lot of trouble seeing past my weight. Remember?"

"Yeah." I remembered. I had thought she was going to die, she was so skinny then. She would never eat, and once she'd fainted when we were in the shopping mall.

"The trouble wasn't with my weight; the trouble was with my feelings. I liked going with Allan because I didn't have to have any real feelings with him; I couldn't handle feelings then. I didn't know what I felt. Everything I felt turned into feeling fat. I had this strong obsession that if I could only look good, everything else would be fine. If I looked good, I'd be happy, accepted, admired and powerful. Only first I had to get rid of all the fat."

"You weren't fat," I protested. She'd been so skinny I used to think she'd collapse if she had to walk from one end of the school to the other.

"No, but I thought I was."

I'd almost forgotten what it had been like then. She used to talk about diets, fat and food all the time and weigh herself three or four times in a day. "It seems a long time ago now."

"Yeah, thank God. It was pretty hard at the time."

"I didn't really know what you were going through. I guess I was busy and . . . ." I looked sideways at her apologetically. "Blind."

"It wasn't your fault. I kept everything secret." She tossed a pebble into the air and caught it. "Dad helped me a lot."

"Your dad? He's so quiet." Mr. Jennings didn't seem to me to be a sensitive man. Nice guy. Polite. But I couldn't see him erupting with emotions the way my dad did, laughing, swearing or playing the bagpipes. It was hard to imagine he'd understand the need to do all those things.

"He told me that he hadn't learned to talk about his feelings and that he and Mom had a hard time discussing anything that really mattered and they thought they had taught me how to . . . what did he call it? 'Shove every damn thing down deep.'"

I remembered that Paula had been unhappy and that we hadn't done much together in the eighth grade. I'd never really known what had happened to make the old bubbly Paula come back.

"He told me that if I'd help him to talk about his feelings, he'd help me talk about mine."

I stared at her. Her eyes were bright with tears.

"He loves you?"

"True." She smiled. "He loves me. And then Mom." Paula shook her head. "Mom took me blueberry picking back up into the old clear-cut behind your place. Know it?"

I nodded. I knew it. We usually got berries there. Not this year, though. This year I didn't have time to pick berries.

"She got me two miles from home and then she said that she wanted to talk to me and it was very difficult for her and would I please listen to her all the way through. Then she told me the same thing Dad did." Paula smiled and bit her lower lip. "I cried a lot then because I understood at that moment how much I loved her too. I told her she might practise talking with Dad because he wanted the same thing."

"You mean your mom didn't know that your dad had talked to you and your dad didn't know that your mom had?"

"Right."

"Oh, man. They *really* weren't talking."

"We're all a lot better today."

I held out my hand and she passed me some pebbles. I tossed them into the lake one after another and listened to the plop as they dropped straight down. A kingfisher darted past with a raucous squawk. A squirrel raced along a pine branch, chattering opinions at us. Paula hadn't been able to talk about her feelings, hadn't known what she felt.

"So," I said. "How do you feel about Mike?"

Paula laughed. "Mike is a challenge. I like him. He also irritates me at times. I'm not sure how much I feel for him, but I have a definite interest in him."

"Are you sure?" I couldn't understand it.

"Mike's grown up a lot, Karen. Didn't you notice?"

"I guess. He just isn't as tall or as strong-looking as . . . ." I glanced at Paula.

"Yes?" she said wickedly. "As Kevin perhaps?"

"Okay. I admit that I find Kevin attractive. But that doesn't mean. . . . " I let my voice trail away as I stared out over the water. "Paula." I turned to her. "You understand people so much better than I do. You understand what their feelings are and what yours are. I'm confused. I'm not sure what I feel, much less what other people feel."

"I don't understand everyone. I sure can't figure out why anyone would poison calves. I'm not much on psychopaths, child molesters or rapists." Paula scooted off the log we'd been sitting on, stood and wiped her hands on her jeans.

I scrambled after her and stood beside her on the bank. "Okay. But you understand our friends better than I do. You understand guys better."

"Maybe. I guess climbing out of that obsession with my looks forced me to understand at least my own feelings most of the time. I don't know. I wouldn't say I was any expert. I *look* for feelings maybe more than you do."

She walked over to Sheeba, picked up the reins and shoved her foot into the stirrup. "So?" she said as she swung her foot over the saddle. "How do you feel about Kevin?"

I bit my lip, thought for a moment, then shook my head and threw up my hands.

She laughed, kicked her heels into Sheeba's sides and trotted off into the trees.

I wasn't totally ignorant. I knew some things. I knew the messages Kevin sent to me came from his feelings, and the ones he got from me came from mine. We must have oceans of feelings, rages, fears and loves someplace inside us. Paula hadn't talked about them and she'd paid for her silence with a sick body. Was I like that? Did I set up barriers in my mind so I wouldn't know that I hated, feared and loved? Kevin sent waves of feelings toward me, past those barriers and into my head. Maybe that was the only way he could get through.

Chapter 8

Paula had aced the judging competition at our 4-H show. Somehow, she'd picked the points the judges wanted to hear and written them all down. I shouldn't have been surprised. Paula wanted to go to Vancouver. When she decides to do something, she usually does it.

Paula, Sarah and I, two other 4-H members, Mrs. Jennings and Kevin rode down to Vancouver in Mrs. Jennings' van. Kevin drove. Mrs. Jennings was happy to have help with the driving.

"I'll come back with my brother so he can help Dad and me get in the wood next week," Kevin had told me when I found out he was going to be with us.

"And you'll get four days in Vancouver without paying your way down."

"I'll throw in some money for gas."

"She won't take it." We both knew Mrs. Jennings.

It took us six hours to drive from the rolling grasslands, lodge-pole pine and open spaces of the Cariboo to a different world of tall trees, ferns and humid air. As we neared the city the traffic increased until we were crammed in a line of cars and trucks inching slowly over a high bridge. Grey and dark brown concrete and wooden buildings in disjointed patterns lay beneath us, where warehouses, industrial plants and transportation depots competed for space along the flatlands beside the river.

We drove through the city to the very centre to the Pacific National Exhibition grounds. I'd expected the grounds to be full of crowded buildings and concrete, but what I found was open space and a view of the Coast Mountains, dark blue against the clear afternoon sky. After miles of buildings, traffic lights and noise, those mountains looked like clean air, solitude and a promise of escape from the city. I had just arrived and I was looking for a way out.

Mrs. Jennings stayed a few miles away with her cousin. Kevin went to his brother's apartment downtown, while the rest of us bunked at the dorm on the exhibition grounds. We left our duffel bags in our rooms, picked up our instruction sheets and headed for the barns.

The fair had been running for a week, but the 4-H exhibition part of it had just begun. Each of us was assigned to a livestock club to help with the cleanup and neatness of its stalls, make friends and "learn by doing." Experience was supposed to teach us competence. I was assigned to the Matsqui Holstein Club — dairy cows. I knew almost nothing about dairy cows except that they looked like starved versions of beef cattle, but I was grateful that the organizers hadn't given me to a chicken club. Paula was placed near me at the Clearbrook Ayrshire Club, also dairy cows. She, too, was happy to avoid a chicken club.

"Or a rabbit club," she said, wincing.

"A rabbit wouldn't seem to be a big enough 4-H project, would it?" I said.

"No." Paula thought for a moment. "Do you think we're prejudiced? I mean, people do make a living raising rabbits. Rabbits have breed characteristics and preferred qualities. You'd have to watch feed costs and market prices the same way we do with beef, so why do rabbits seem to be a little kid's project?"

"We *are* prejudiced," I said. "You're right. We come from beef country and we think our projects are better."

"Disgusting, aren't we?" Paula said cheerfully.

"Absolutely," I agreed.

Sarah joined the Langley Lamb Club. I showed her my

compound first so she knew how to find me if she needed me, then I took her to the Langley compound and made sure there was an adult in charge.

"I'll be back in an hour to take you to supper," I said.

"Don't be late. I'm hungry."

I promised not to forget her and left.

I worked with the Matsqui club, doing all the practical, routine jobs that had to be done. I like the physical chores of farming, and I sometimes wonder if I could be happy just working as a farm hand. But I love science, and life as a veterinarian would combine science and hard work. Mom keeps urging me to take more English courses at school because she says I have an "intellectual and emotional appreciation of language," but I don't think I would be happy thinking, reading and studying all the time. I like to be active. Shovelling out stalls and feeding cows feels good.

By the time all the work on the stall had been completed, I had met all the Matsqui 4-H members and their chaperons and was part of the group.

When Paula and I approached Sarah to take her to supper, she was sitting on a hay bale with her feet hanging over the sides while the other kids were working. I frowned at her.

"Why aren't you helping?"

"I'm supposed to stay here for another five minutes," she said. Sarah was not happy.

I found the chaperon in the tack room.

"Hi," I said. "I'm Karen Stewartson, Sarah's sister. Is there a problem?"

"Oh, hi." The short, blond woman shook my hand. "I'm Suzanne. Not really a problem, no, but I told Sarah not to leave the stall unless she asked me, and she ran off to get herself a pop without checking in. This is the big city and she is only ten."

"Oh, yeah. Well, she does listen if she thinks you mean it," I said, "but she is impulsive. Maybe I should keep popping over here."

"No, don't worry about her. I've raised four sons. There isn't anything she could dream up that one of my sons didn't try."

I laughed. Suzanne smiled.

"Don't give her another thought. Jail would seem permissive compared to my little area of control here. I think she got the message that I'm in charge."

"Great," Paula said as we walked toward Sarah. "Someone with the combined personality of a Girl Scout leader, a prison warden and a school principal. Just the person to understand Sarah."

We sat down on the hay bale on either side of Sarah.

"We'll stay with you until your sentence is over. Then you can come to supper with us."

Sarah picked at the hay and shredded a piece between her fingers. She peeked over at the kids who were still putting down bedding and feeding sheep.

"Uh, Karen?"

"Yeah?"

"Do you think I should stay and help the other kids until everything is done?"

I tried not to show shock. "Probably," I said. This helpful, thoughtful girl was my sister?

"Maybe I could go to supper with them, if Suzanne says I can."

I nodded. "Sounds like a good idea, Squirt. See you later."

Paula and I hopped off the bale and scooted for the cafeteria before Sarah changed her mind. We stopped outside the door.

"Yes!" I said, and hit Paula a high-five. This trip to the city was going to be a holiday for me!

When we returned from supper, Kevin and his brother, Bob, stood near the Matsqui Holstein Club sign. Bob, three years older than Kevin, was taking his last year at the university. He had stayed in the city for the summer, but was going home with Kevin to help cut and haul the winter firewood. Kevin says Bob doesn't want to ranch; he wants to be a teacher, but he works with his dad and Kevin when they need him. He hadn't been a part of 4-H during high school, and I didn't know him well. I didn't know the girl with them either.

"Hi, Kev," Paula said. "Hi, Bob."

"Hi, Paula," Kevin said, but he looked at me.

I'd seen him just hours ago. He was still in the uniform of the Cariboo: jeans, T-shirt, leather jacket and Stetson, but he looked different here in the barns — older and taller somehow. Bob introduced his friend, Sheila. I glanced at her. I had never seen anyone so skinny, unless it was Paula when she was in trouble with her eating disorder. I'd never seen anyone with a shaved head before either. Some of the girls in our school wore their hair really short, but no one had shaved all the hair from their head. Maybe this term someone would. Sheila had a gold stud in her nose and three or four in her ears. She looked experienced and a little bored. She also looked as if she knew everything I didn't. I wondered if all the university women were like her.

"Hi," I said.

She said hi and looked around. "These are cows," she said as if she'd made a great discovery. Kevin and I nodded. Bob just grinned.

Paula started to walk away. "I'm going out with my stall-mates tonight. We're hitting the midway, so I'd better catch them before they leave without me."

"Are you sure, Paula?" I called after her. "You can come with us."

"I'm fine," she said. "Truly. And you're no fun on the midway."

She was right about that. Midway rides scared me. I didn't see any sense in climbing onto a midway ride and inviting fear. Kevin knew I liked the sounds, smells and the excitement of a midway, but the ferris wheel was about all I wanted to experience. As far as I was concerned, "Learning by doing" didn't apply to the midway.

We stood in the alleyway between the rows of animals, watching Paula walk away. Bob and Sheila looked like posed models with the rows of cows behind them, the up-scale couple in front of the "rural scene." Bob probably wanted a girlfriend who couldn't stand farming.

"Are you from Vancouver, Sheila?"

She nodded and looked over her shoulder at me. "Yes, right downtown in the city. Vancouver born, bred, educated and socialized. Buses, noise, people. None of this." She flicked her hand at the cows.

I felt disgustingly wholesome for a moment. Sheila was so different from me. She had shaved her head bald, layered on the mascara and hid any figure she had in a long black sweater that ended at the top of high leather boots. I tried to imagine myself in her place, and couldn't.

"Have you seen anything of the fair yet?" Bob asked me.

I shook my head.

Kevin leaned closer. I could smell the leather from his jacket and the spice of his shampoo. "Can you get off now?"

"Just a minute, I'll find out." Kevin stood beside me and listened while I spoke with the chaperon. She told me I was free until eight the next morning, when she wanted me to help with the milking, but not to forget to be in the dorm by midnight.

I picked up my jacket and walked away from the compound toward Sheila and Bob.

"Kevin, I've never milked a cow."

"You'll do okay," he said. "They probably use electric milking machines, so you'll only have to hook it up."

"I guess they would. I can deal with machinery, but I hope the cows are patient."

"They're 4-H cows," Kevin said.

True. They would be used to people.

He looked around the barn. "Have you seen any good beef?"

"Actually, I haven't had time to explore. Do you want to do that now?"

"Yeah. I hear there's a good line of Charolais here from Kamloops. Dad was thinking that we might get better production pound per head at a lower cost if we bred some of their line into our Herefords." We were standing beside Bob and Sheila by now, so stopped talking and turned to them.

"I'm not looking at cattle," Bob said.

Sheila wrinkled her nose. "Me either. Definitely not my world, not even cooked."

She was a vegetarian? I glanced quickly at Bob, but didn't say anything. I looked down at her leather boots — she didn't eat it; she wore it — but still, I didn't say anything.

"Why don't we meet you guys in an hour at the roller coaster?" Bob moved his feet impatiently.

Kevin raised his eyebrows in a question. I nodded. "Okay," he said.

I watched Bob and Sheila walk down the alley between the rows of animals. Sheila looked like a parrot in a hen yard, as out of place here as I would be in the university crowd. It was a depressing thought. How was I going to manage next year and all seven years after that if I didn't belong in that world? The light glinted off her long earrings, then she and Bob disappeared behind a group of 4-H kids.

Kevin tugged my hand. "Come on. Let's go."

We headed first for the Charolais display that Kevin

wanted to see. We talked about production costs and types of beef cattle while we looked at the different animals on display.

Not only 4-H members had their animals at the exhibition. Breeders from all over the province came to compete for the best Charolais cow with calf, the best Ayrshire milking cow or the best Holstein heifer.

A couple of the men standing beside the Charolais talked to us about their breeding programs. We both asked questions because I was interested and I knew Dad wanted the information. We had a couple of Charolais cows, but didn't use that breed of bull. Charolais took more feed, but the men tried to show us how we could make more money in sales after factoring in the cost of feed.

Kevin had more detailed questions than I did because his dad was getting close to buying a Charolais bull. I stood quietly and thought about the reasons for raising cows. Was it just money? If we were only after money, then we should sell land, sell the lakeside property to Andy Foster and take the money. Dad and Mom wanted to make money so they could continue to ranch, so they could continue to live where we lived, so I could go to university and Sarah could have music lessons and we could have what we needed to be happy.

"Is anyone trying to buy your ranch?" I asked the two men when they had finished their comments on the bull.

The older man looked at me quickly. "Yes. There's a developer trying to get us to sell. I guess the folks down here at the Coast are looking for summer cabins."

"Is anyone selling?" Kevin asked.

"A few."

"What's the name of the company?" Maybe Andy Foster's efforts to buy our ranch was something I needed to understand better. I wasn't sure why I was asking these questions, but I wanted the answers.

"Don't remember." The man looked at his friend, but the friend shook his head. "Sorry. I think the developers were from up your way, but I just don't remember what they called themselves."

"Foster Realty?" I suggested.

He shook his head.

I remembered the men's comments at the dance. "Shandon Developers?"

The man smiled. "Sorry. Don't remember."

"Thanks anyway." I nodded and stepped back.

Kevin wrote down his dad's name and address, told the men to call and took their business card. Then we had a quick look at everything we could before we met Bob and Sheila. Sheila was easy to spot. Her shaved head and bright bronze earrings stood out, even in this crowd.

The twilight was long here, the daylight fading slowly as the coloured midway lights grew brighter. Crowds of people moved in eddying circles around barkers, carrying us with them and then leaving us outside the current, watching others. The air smelled of popcorn, fried onions and dust.

"This is really crazy, Kevin," I said as we stood in line for the roller coaster.

"Very crazy," Sheila said behind me. "But fun." She winked at me. "It's one of the few times I get to be scared, dependent and in need of hugs."

"Oh," I said, getting a new perspective on roller coaster rides, and on Sheila. Suddenly I smiled at her. Her eyes lit and she laughed.

Kevin squeezed my hand, but didn't say anything. I think he was having second thoughts about committing our healthy bodies to this dangerous ride.

"It looks so old." I glanced at the sleigh-like contraption as we climbed in.

"About thirty years old," Bob said. "Mom and Dad rode on it."

"Oh, God. I'm going to die," Sheila said dramatically. I glanced at her, startled for a moment, before I saw that her eyes were laughing.

The wooden cart creaked and groaned as it began to move over the thin metal rails. It felt as if the whole structure was going to fly into pieces. The first part of the ride was unnerving, but tolerable. We clanked up a steep incline, the beams and crossbars underneath sighing and shifting.

"They must have inspected it. Wouldn't they do that, Kev? I mean, somebody must care about being sued?" I definitely shouldn't be on this. It was a crazy idea. I was going to die of fright if I didn't actually die in a crash.

"Sure," he said. "It's safe enough." He paused for a moment, then added, "It doesn't feel safe, though, does it?"

I was going to agree with him, but didn't have time. The car slid over the crest and careened down the other side, then whipped around a ninety-degree turn. My stomach stayed at the first turn, and I grabbed the steel bar holding us in.

We were out of control, shooting into space and doomed to die. I knew it. This was the stupidest thing I had ever done in my life!

I felt Kevin's arms around me. I let go of the bar and glued myself to his chest. The short ride seemed to go on for hours. We shot down another drop, spun around a couple more turns and then coasted to a stop. When I was sure we were no longer moving, I released my grip on Kevin's waist, peeled myself off his chest and climbed stiffly from the car. I walked slowly down the exit path. Sheila bounced past me.

"That wasn't so bad, was it?"

"It was," I said solemnly, "very bad." I was not going to pretend courage here. She laughed. Bob walked past me, slipped his arm around Sheila's shoulders and gave her a hug. "What's next?" I groaned.

"You guys go on the wild rides without us," Kevin said. "Karen will only get sick and barf all over us."

I was going to protest, but decided to stay honest. "Hey, it's true."

Kevin hugged me. "She's a real wimp. We'll check out the merry-go-round." We all agreed that I was a wimp and a drop-out on the midway scene.

Kevin and I traipsed around the midway, watching Sheila and Bob spend a lot of money on rides. They rode the Scream Machine and the Zipper and Ring of Fire where they hung upside down at the top of a huge circle. It was fun to watch them, but I didn't want to join them. They didn't ride the Ejection Seat because it cost eighty dollars. Why would anyone ride it, even if it were free? Two people sat strapped into seats in the middle of a round cage. They were winched up between tall towers, but held back by a hook on a crane beneath them. When they reached a certain height, the hook released and, on the principle of a slingshot, they flew into the air and were flung around the sky like plastic crash dolls, then fell back held only by the bungee cords attached to the towers. That was supposed to be fun?

"I think you'd have to have a death wish to get into that," Bob said.

"And money," Sheila added. "You'd feel great when it was over, though. Wouldn't it be wild?"

We watched the demolition derby for a while. The noise was tremendous as cars roared around the track and banged into each other. It was weird and somehow exciting to see cars deliberately wrecked. I kept looking to make sure they were real cars with real people in them. No one was hurt, but it looked as if they were going to be at any second.

Later we sat on a park bench eating cotton candy and watching people stroll by. The organ music from the merry-go-round mixed with the sounds of barkers calling for anyone to try to win a stuffed pig and the bingo announcer calling letters. Somewhere a band played, but I was too tired to go look for it.

"Hey." I glanced at my watch. "I've got a midnight curfew."

"It's quarter to," Kevin said. "We'd better go."

"We'll wait here," Bob said, helping himself to Sheila's cotton candy. "You take her back."

Sheila waved the cotton candy at us. "See you again."

"Yeah," I smiled at her. "I hope so."

Hand in hand, Kevin and I ran for the dorm.

It was five minutes to midnight when we reached the sidewalk in front of the door.

"I have to go home tomorrow. Bob has only ten days off and Mom wants him home now."

"There goes your four-day holiday."

"Yeah, but I have a lot to do at home anyway before we go for firewood."

"You don't mind driving down to the coast one day and driving back the next?"

"No, not really. Dad and Bob and I will be camping out in the bush for a week, and Mom wants some time with Bob. It's okay."

"Then in two weeks you'll drive back here to university."

"Yeah. Well, I'll probably be driving back and forth quite a bit." He reached for my hands and drew me closer. "I'll see you before I leave home, but we won't have much time."

True. We wouldn't see much of each other if he was going to spend a week cutting firewood. I looked up at him. "I had a great time tonight."

He slipped his hands around my waist.

"I'm sure going to miss you, Kay." I felt him kiss the top of my head. "One quick visit before I leave for school and then I won't see you until Thanksgiving."

I hugged him. "Yeah."

"How about a kiss to keep me sane for the next week?"

"Good idea."

It was another of those mind-blowing kisses. It scrambled my brains, melted my bones and was as exhilarating as the roller coaster ride. I took a deep breath, drew back and started down the walk. At the front door I stopped and turned to him. "Kevin?"

"Yeah." He was standing where I left him.

"Don't practise any more," I called softly. "You're too much already."

His low laugh wrapped around me like warm air and sunshine, sending me smiling through the door on the stroke of midnight.

Chapter 9

I had a great time at the exhibition — competing, working and talking. My new 4-H friends spoke to me about their lives and their problems. Paula and I traded comments on what we were doing and the people we met. Fairgoers stopped and asked questions about the dairy cows and about farming.

Occasionally, I'd think about the development company in Kamloops and Andy Foster and what he might do to our land. I looked at the houses stacked one on another on the land around Vancouver and shuddered. I didn't want that in the Cariboo.

The exhibition included other animals as strange as llamas and as familiar as pigs. Separate buildings held all kinds of farm equipment, as well as the food fair and a home show. Buskers walked the midway and stood outside the agricultural buildings, juggling coloured balls and telling jokes. There was even a nightly rodeo.

I didn't win the demonstration competition. Sarah didn't win her class either, but Paula did well in the judging, despite having to adjudicate chickens.

"They all look the same," she told me. "Nervous, complaining twits. I couldn't see why any one of them was better than another. And I was only bullshitting the breeds. Can *you* tell a Rhode Island Red from a Red Leghorn?"

I shook my head.

"I gave it my best guess," she said.

While Paula didn't know poultry, she knew beef and lambs very well. She kept her average judging score high and came home with a trophy.

We slept most of the way home, tired from the constant stimulation of many people and much noise. I woke just before we turned up the Misty Lake road and watched the moonlight and shadows play on the pine trees and grasses in the open meadows. On the curve above Paula's place, I saw the glimmer of moonlight on the bay, silver and shimmering, then we rolled down the hill to the ranch. My lake. My woods. Home.

Sarah stirred a little on my lap. When she is tired, scared or lonely, Sarah remembers that I carried her and cuddled her when she was a toddler, and that I love her. At those times I remember it too. She is sweet then, and precious.

In the morning it seemed as if I'd never been away. The ranch looked the same and all the animals as I had left them. Mom remained at Grandma's, but hoped to come home soon.

I was putting away the breakfast dishes when I heard a motorbike. From the porch window I saw Trevor Foster get off his bike and unsnap his helmet. Dad walked across the yard, stopped in front of him, talked to him and then motioned him to stay where he was.

"What's he doing here?" I said when Dad opened the back door. I had the phone in my hand, ready to call Will Fraser.

"He's putting in one hundred community hours at our place."

"Here? At our ranch?" I stared in disbelief.

Dad nodded.

How could this happen? I knew first offenders usually received a sentence of community service. No probation. No jail. No record. Just community labour for a specified number of supervised hours. I hadn't asked Dad what the judge had given Trevor and his friends. I assumed it would be community service, that was usual and even predictable, but I hadn't guessed the court would assign him to our ranch. "He's doing those hours here?" I asked, stunned by the idea.

"Yeah." Dad looked on the kitchen counter. "I need a pencil and some paper."

I reached blindly into a drawer beside the sink and mechanically handed him both. I felt heat rise in my body. "That's putting a fox in the hen house, isn't it?" I snapped.

"He has to go somewhere. I said I'd take him." Dad looked at me sternly. I glared back at him.

"He threatened Sarah."

"Look, Karen," he said. "I'll deal with him."

"Sarah and I have to deal with him too. He'll be here, won't he?"

"He starts tomorrow. You and Sarah will be in no danger. He doesn't want to be here any more than you want him here, but he's coming, he's staying and it's going to be a good experience for everyone." Dad spoke in his *I am the father and don't sass me* voice.

I bit my lip. "Why didn't you tell me he was coming?"

Dad moved to the back door. "Because I didn't want you to get worried about it ahead of time . . . "

"Protecting the little girls in your family?" I wasn't often sarcastic, but I was really angry now.

Dad ignored that. " . . . and because there wasn't anything you could do about it. I'd already promised the court that I'd take him. I'm sorry if you think I should have asked you, but you were away and I had to make the decision. I know you can handle it. You're always reasonable and fair."

I wasn't impressed. "Oh, sure. Try flattery."

He smiled at me and waited. I thought for a moment. Dad had already committed himself to looking after Trevor; that meant he had committed all of us.

"Trevor's going to do something wild. He's self-centred, self-serving and nasty. He should at least be punished for harassing our cows, not given a gentle slap like this. Community service is too soft."

Dad leaned against the doorjamb. "Community service works best. Our success rate at preventing young people from becoming criminals is better with this system than with a punishing one."

"Really?" I didn't believe it.

"Really. In spite of what you read in the newspapers, our crimes are down when we use a way that keeps kids out of the criminal justice system."

It didn't seem reasonable to me, or fair. "So you're helping the statistics?"

"No," he said patiently. "I'm helping kids. Anyway, there are very few men who haven't done something pretty stupid in their past. I'd hate to have been hit with the justice system for what I did."

Dad? In trouble with the law? "What did you do?"

"Don't spread it around town, but I stole a car when I was fifteen. The rancher I stole it from didn't report me. He made me repair it and remake the motor. It took me every Saturday for six months." He paused for a moment, staring out the window. Then he shrugged and half smiled. "To me, kids like Trevor look just like the kid I was."

I nodded, recognizing his point. I could now understand why he had volunteered to take Trevor, but I still thought he was wrong. Trevor was trouble. Capital T. Guaranteed.

"Trust me," Dad said as he returned to Trevor to arrange the days and hours of his work.

I didn't even want to think about Trevor or how I felt about him. I had plenty of work to distract me. The post office had sent a replacement worker to deliver the mail when I had been away, so as there was no delivery over the weekend, I was free until Monday. At least, I had thought I was free until I climbed into my truck on Friday evening to take Sarah over to Heather's. When I opened the door, I saw a small bit of white paper stuffed between the back cushion and the seat.

"Hold it, Sarah."

She stood at the door of the truck while I pried the cushions apart and pulled the paper out — a letter for Mr. Jennings.

"Uh-oh," Sarah said. "Mom always delivers the mail on the day she gets it." She sounded smug and pious.

I studied the letter, then put it on the dash. "I know. I must have missed it the Monday before we left for Vancouver."

"Hah!" Sarah said with satisfaction. "It's *really* late then."

"Okay, okay, it's late." She is younger than I am; she is unthinking; I will not snap at her no matter how much she asks for it. I repeated this litany to myself, hoping it would help.

"If you wait until Monday to deliver it, it will be over a week late," she said with irritating accuracy.

"I know."

"You'll make Mom look bad at the post office."

That was it. I'd had it. "Sarah! I'll deliver it tonight. Now lay off!"

She liked it when I did something wrong. Somehow, it made her feel more equal or superior or something. I dropped her at Heather's, spoke to Mary Jane for a few moments about the exhibition and then drove back to the Jennings' house.

Mrs. Jennings took the letter from me at her back door. "Not to worry, Karen. It's just a letter from Foster Realty. That man is always asking for a listing to sell our ranch."

"Yeah. He asks us too." I wondered again if he was

buying up the ranches in the Kamloops area as well. What did he do with all that land? Resell it? Did he have that many customers? Was he working for someone else?

"I don't know how many times we have to say 'No' to him to make him believe it."

"Well, even so, Mrs. Jennings, I'm sorry I didn't include it in Monday's mail. It just slipped behind the seat of my truck and I didn't see it."

"No problem. No problem." She tucked the letter into her jeans pocket. "You should stop at the barn and see Paula. She's giving Junebug a little extra attention tonight because we're turning all the cattle out on the lease range tomorrow, including Junebug." We exchanged a look of understanding. Paula would not want to let Junebug go.

The lease range was west of the Jennings' ranch: lodge-pole pine, rolling hills and a good place for grass at this time of year. We had a similar lease to the east of our place, with two small lakes for water and a new-growth forest — good cattle country. Paula would have mixed feelings about sending Junebug out with the cattle. On the one hand, Junebug would get grass with high protein and good nutrition, and, of course, access to the bull. On the other hand, she would lose her friendliness and become wary of people. I had turned Edie out this morning on our lease land, but I hadn't conducted a ritualistic parting scene or drowned the whole event with emotion the way I knew Paula would.

The sun was low behind me as I entered the barn. Sunset took a long time this far north, and the yellow evening light lent a luminous beauty to the barn. The boards seemed a richer brown; the steel hinges glinted sparks. The rays of sunshine slanting through the loft window lit the barn with a soft glow so that even the dust on the top of the feed bins looked golden brown.

Paula was in the last stall, brushing Junebug's back.

Shafts of light moved in a pattern of bronze, dark red and black shadows as the brush moved up and down over the calf's coat. Music from the radio floated softly on the air — classical strings; Junebug didn't like loud rock. Paula sang in a kind of a chant, "You're going out to meet the bull, the bull. You're going out to meet the bull." Then, "Pregnant at two. Pregnant at two."

"Hi," I said as I slid through the gate and leaned against the wall.

"Hi." She looked at me briefly, just enough for me to see the sheen of tears in her eyes, and then turned back to Junebug.

"So, Paula, how can you raise a calf to have only one purpose in life?"

"I know. I can't believe I'm part of such a sexist scheme."

We smiled at each other. There wasn't any romance in the world of bulls and cows. All their matings seemed to be without any thought or even special attention. Cows were concerned about their calves — they watched for them, called them and looked for them when they were lost. They even had babysitting groups where one cow looked after several calves for a time during the day, but I'd never seen a cow show any concern or emotion for a bull.

"Cows and bulls don't really like each other much, do they?" I said.

"They don't seem to."

"There are couples like that, don't you think, Paula? They may be partners, but they don't like each other?"

She smoothed Junebug's coat with her hand and glanced at me. "Yeah. Lots of them."

"Scary, isn't it?"

"Yeah. Like Bryan Tyeson and his wife, Lydia. Did you see them at the dance?"

I thought back to the night of the 4-H dance. "I saw

them, but I didn't notice anything odd about them."

"I was pouring myself some juice when they were getting food during the supper hour. They were arguing." Paula leaned her back against Junebug's side.

"About what?"

"It was a picky-picky kind of sniping. You could just tell that they wanted to irritate each other." She pushed her voice into a high squeak imitating Lydia. "You've got the emotional depth of a calculator."

Then she growled, "I'm not a weeping mess, that's for sure."

I could see Tyeson in my mind then: tall, thin, dressed in his western shirt and jeans, standing by the food table, leaning down a little to listen to his wife, her smooth blond hair swinging back as she spoke, his face momentarily grave, his eyes serious. I had noticed them.

Paula resumed the high voice. "Of course not. You aren't the least bit sensitive, are you?"

"Ugh!" Paula said in her normal voice. "People who don't like each other should not marry."

"That's profound, Paula."

"That's me," Paula said. "The guru of Misty Lake."

Junebug shifted and Paula adjusted her weight until she was comfortable again. I leaned against the stall gate.

"I think Lydia drinks," I said. Mom had told me that. "After her son died, I think she got worse and now has a real problem."

"Maybe she didn't like Mr. Tyeson to start with."

I could see the dance floor in my mind. "And Andy Foster was there alone because he's been divorced for three years."

"Yeah, right. There are lots of divorced people in our town. The divorce rate is almost as high as the marriage rate. Look at the parents of the kids in our class. Most of them are divorced."

I squatted down with my back against the wall, picked up a piece of hay and twirled it between my fingers. Seeds flew onto the floor and into the dirt in the cracks. "So, tell me, Paula. Do you think the cows have it right? I mean, should we just get together with guys to produce children and then ignore men the rest of the time? A sort of 'Come home with me, you're handy' approach?"

"If we do it with the principles of animal science," Paula said, "we should first look at their bloodlines and doctor's report — like a pedigree and vet check."

"Sounds reasonable," I said, interested. Paula sometimes had fantastic ideas. She warmed to the idea of uncommitted coupling.

"When you look at the way people split up, it looks like animal behaviour is the next step for us. Momentary satisfaction. No commitment. I mean, so many women bring up kids by themselves anyway, maybe we should look at the way cows live. Have a kid and dump it on society in a year and then have another."

"You mean only commit to children for a couple of years, the way cows do? The way they have calves, nurse them, then leave them?"

"Simple, isn't it?" Paula said. "No men to help raise them, so keep them for a couple of years and then drop them on society. Let the herd look after them."

I knew she wasn't serious, but I couldn't help but point out a big flaw in her proposal. "It wouldn't work for you, Paula. You're crying tonight because you have to say good-bye to Junebug. Do you think you could let a child go?"

"Oh, no." She turned back to Junebug. "You're right. Not me."

I watched her brush Junebug's coat again and run her hands over the calf's back.

The light in the barn was paler now, shadows grew, the overhead light seemed harsher and shone in the black of

Paula's curls, leaving her eyes in the shadows. She leaned over Junebug's head. "Cows have it easy, don't they Junebug? Bulls can come and go; owners can come and go. No problem. You'll be fine. I'm going to let you out with all the cattle and you'll forget all about me."

I didn't argue. Junebug would forget Paula; at least, her attachment to Paula would diminish. Every year we sent out calves with our love and every year they came back barely remembering us. The trouble is, *we* didn't forget them, but I didn't agonize over the parting the way Paula did.

Junebug turned her head and licked Paula's face. Paula laughed and then cried a little. "She's such a sweetheart. I hate to see her go." She patted Junebug's head.

I felt the tears I hadn't shed for Edie sting at the back of my eyes. I stood, dropped the hay and dusted my hands on my jeans. "I let Edie out this morning."

Paula sniffed. "You don't care the way I do."

First Sarah and now Paula. I didn't need this. "Look. I have some feelings."

She ignored me. I tried to reason with her.

"Come on, Paula. Junebug will like it out there with the cattle once she gets used to it, and you have another calf ready to work on. You know that."

"Shut up, Karen. It's like telling a mother she has other kids. This is the one that's important now."

"Okay. Okay." I may not understand people's feelings all the time, but I sometimes think that Paula has too *many* feelings.

Paula scratched Junebug on her topknot and patted her neck.

"I feel as if I'm sending my kid to college."

"I hope my Mom doesn't feel like this when I go."

"She might be glad to get rid of you."

"That's not true! She loves me, and I love her. So you shut up, Paula." We were arguing like ten-year-olds, chipping away at each other with sharp words.

She cocked her head to the side and looked at me. "Did I hear you actually admit that you have some feelings?"

I took a deep breath. "Paula!"

"I'm sorry," she said. "I know she loves you. I love you myself."

My anger disappeared suddenly, like the air from a burst bubble. We were quiet for a moment, letting the soft twilight soothe us.

I walked behind Paula as she led Junebug to the gate of the near pasture. Tomorrow morning, she and her dad would move all the cattle from that pasture onto the lease range. Paula slipped the halter from Junebug's head and slapped her on the rump. Junebug jerked, took a couple of steps away, but then turned and looked back. Paula closed the gate and leaned on it. Junebug came to the gate and hung her head over Paula's hands.

"See you tomorrow, sweetie," Paula whispered.

"Want me to stay for a while?" I asked as we walked back to the barnyard.

"No. I'm going to get out some 'hurtin' song' tapes and maybe some old movies, and cry for a couple of hours."

"Okay." When Paula felt depressed, she wallowed in it. "Enjoy yourself." I climbed into my truck and leaned out the window. "How's everything with you and Mike?"

Paula stood nearer. Her eyes sparkled a little and she almost smiled. "Kind of exciting."

"Mike? I can't believe it. Our Mike?"

"The same," Paula said.

I shook my head. "Remember him trying out for the baseball team in tenth grade — twenty pounds overweight?"

"In case you haven't noticed, that extra weight has gone into his shoulders."

I was silent for a moment, thinking about Mike as I'd seen him in the hayfields this summer. "He *is* good looking in a way. Are you getting serious?"

Paula looked back toward the pasture where Junebug was still leaning on the gate. "I'm not sure I'm ready for Mike. He's going to school in Alberta next week. I'll be here. Maybe that will make it easier to talk more and feel less."

"You mean talking is enough?" I was seriously starting to doubt that. Kissing Kevin could become addictive. Reasoning, planning and responsible action were beginning to seem less operative in my life.

"Well, no. I'm just saying it isn't always a good idea for me to use my body to express myself."

I stared at her. "You sound like my Mom. 'Safe sex is no sex.'"

She looked worried for a moment. I felt contrite. She didn't need criticism any more than I did. "The thing is, Paula, maybe that's right for you. Maybe it's even right for me. I guess we each have to work out that for ourselves. You know, do whatever suits us best."

She nodded. "There isn't any other way, is there?"

I felt a little stupid. "I guess not, if we can ever figure out what it is we want and need."

"Yeah."

"And everything around us seems to change all the time."

"That too," Paula said.

We stood there in silence for a moment, listening to the night sounds. I heard a coyote howl in the hills behind the Jennings' house and a horse whinny from the barn. Junebug raised her chin and complained about being left alone. A snipe fluttered above us, its wings winnowing a drumming sound. I took a deep breath of the cool air. "Have a good cry."

She nodded, stepped back and waved. "See you tomorrow."

Chapter 10

When I was halfway home, I turned between a patch of
scrub willows onto the shortcut, a rough trail almost
straight through the bush to our barn. No one uses it but
people from our ranch and Paula's, so I didn't expect to
see any traffic. I drive it often in the daylight and know
the dips, curves and rough spots well enough to drive without lights.

I shut off the headlights because deer wander onto the
road. I hate it when they freeze in the circle of light, waiting to be hit. They panic; I panic, and either slam my
brakes or try to swerve around them.

The moon painted the trail with patches of pale light,
transforming the greens and yellows of the daylight forest
into blue and grey, as if someone had put a blue filter into
a virtual reality game. Blue pine boughs swept the top of
the truck, grey poplar leaves brushed the sides. In an open
meadow the grass looked almost black with silver stripes
where the moonlight broke through the pines, the patterns
changing slightly as the breeze from the lake stirred the
trees.

I stopped the truck at a spot where I could see the lake
and gazed around me, trying to capture this in my mind
like a photograph: the tall pines, the silver poplars and the
slivers of white birch trunks. I wanted to remember this, a
perfect part of the world where time stopped for a moment to revel in beauty. I leaned out the open window
and smelled the night air. The spice of the pine pitch and
the sweet tang of blueberries mixed with the fresh smell of

grass — another picture I wanted to keep with me forever. The lake curved around the bay and I saw our meadow, a pale square by the water.

I had stared at the moonlight on the meadow for some time before I noticed the pinpricks of light bobbing and weaving through the trees on the other side. I watched for a moment, thinking I was seeing fireflies or some kind of phosphorous bug. But the lights grew bigger and brighter. There were three of them close together, moving toward the meadow down the old mill road.

Bikers.

I slammed the truck into gear and headed for the meadow. Halfway there, common sense caught me. There were three of them, one of me. Confrontation was not smart.

I drove as close as I dared to the meadow, pulled off the road into a grove of trees and cut the engine. The noise of the dirt bikes was loud now. I didn't think they had heard my engine above theirs.

I eased the truck door shut and crept through the trees until I stood behind a big fir at the edge and on the high side of the meadow. The bikes formed a tight circle near the hay shed, their headlights facing in. At that moment, the bike motors died; the lights blinked out. For a second I heard nothing. Then, slowly, the night sounds of the breeze and the birds crept back into the air. A loon cast a crazy incantation into the dark.

One of the bikers spoke. "The cows come here for salt?"

Another answered. "Yeah. They have to have salt. Just spray the stuff over the salt block. That ought to get them for sure."

"Hey, dude, I'll bet you we take down half the herd tonight. One little can, two salt blocks and all that power."

They were poisoning our cattle.

I took a deep breath and told myself to stay where I was. It was still three against one and they were dangerous.

"Pretty good job, tonight. Two hits and we get the herd."

"Maybe," the tall one said. I could see the two bikers who were talking standing by their bikes, silhouetted against the light background of the moonlit lake. The other one sat in darkness on his bike, with his feet splayed out for balance.

"Did you see that cow come right up to me?" one of the standing bikers said. "Opened its mouth and let me put the spray right inside. That shook it. Dumb. That's one cow that's history." He laughed.

No one could get close enough to a cow to hand-feed it. All our cattle were a little wary of people.

Except Edie. Anyone could get close to Edie.

"This is easy, man. Fifty bucks for nothing."

"Let's split," the one on the bike said curtly. He sounded worried. "They might be patrolling this place now."

For a second I thought I recognized Trevor's voice.

"Okay, okay. We're gone."

I saw the tall biker throw something and heard the ping of a can as it hit a rock. They had come, sprayed poison and were leaving in less than two minutes. Fast, efficient and deadly.

They started their engines, revved their motors and headed toward the old mill road. I watched the lights until they disappeared into the trees and stood waiting until I could no longer hear the whine of the bike engines in the air. Where would they have found another salt block? Where would they have found Edie?

I returned to my truck and drove to the hay shed. I left the headlights on and the motor running. Starting at the truck, I searched systematically in a semi-circle, cramming on my fencing gloves as I searched, until, after about five minutes, I saw the can of *Wipe Out*. They'd pitched it about four feet from the salt block. I picked up the can and tossed it onto the floor of the cab. The red salt cube was new — Dad had just put it out yesterday — so it was still a fifty-pound block. I backed the truck until the tailgate was above the block, heaved it onto the floor of the box and shoved it back. I took a piece of fluorescent flagging from the back of the truck, wrapped it around a stick and marked the spot where the salt block had been so that Dad and I could check it in the morning.

I worked quickly, doing what I could to prevent poisonings. But in my mind, a tape played over and over. Where would they have found Edie, if they found her? She would have been wandering around on her own, not a part of the herd yet, curious about her new surroundings and searching out food and water. Maybe they had found one of the other cows. Maybe it was a calf that was curious. It didn't have to be Edie.

Dad usually put another salt block near the beaver pond at the mill site. I took the same trail the bikers had and pulled into the flat, sawdust circle, the same place Kevin and I had parked after the dance. I was lucky and picked out the salt block with my headlights as I drove in. I stopped beside it, lifted it into the back of the truck and shoved it close to the other one, again flagging the spot. I yanked off my gloves and tossed them beside the salt block.

As I started to climb back into the cab, I let my eyes drift over the flat circle of the mill site and saw a bit of white just at the edge of the beam from the headlights. I turned, stared and walked slowly toward it. The white patch evolved into the markings on the side of a Hereford. It was lying on its side, very still.

I squatted beside it and put my hand on its nose. No breath warmed my hand. This one was dead. The body was still warm, but dead. I patted it for a minute, afraid to look at the number on its ear tag, afraid to look at the body very closely, afraid to know. Slowly I reached out and felt for the plastic tag. I turned it up until it caught the light. EC-17. I let it fall. I'd known ever since I heard the biker say he had hand-fed the cow that it would be Edie.

I drove back down the trail. The night was the same — the same moon, the same soft breeze off the lake, the same night sounds of the loon and the snipe. But I was different.

Somewhere inside me a rage began slowly. Those bikers had come, dropped poison in the one place that other cows would be sure to get it, casually killed Edie and then left. They didn't stay to watch her die, to watch her convulse in pain, scream in panic and die. They didn't care. I felt as if a thin layer was cracking in my mind and a volcano was boiling through.

By the time I got home, I was shaking with anger. How could they kill like that? What kind of monsters were they?

I slammed the door of my truck and flew up the steps. Dad and Sarah were watching television when I barged into the living room.

"Look at this!" I waved the can of *Wipe Out* in front of them.

Dad stared at me and pressed the mute button, turning off the sound.

"What?" He kept his eyes on my face.

"This!" I shook the can in front of him. "Those bastards are poisoning our cattle again and they don't care. They just don't care!"

Dad rose from the couch and took the can from me. He stared at it as he listened. Sarah stayed where she was, her eyes big and a little frightened.

"I will not have it anymore!" I screamed at him. "How can they do this? What kind of empty-headed demons are they? Don't they have any compassion? Any understanding? Any humanity? It was probably Trevor. Good old Trev and his friends are poisoning our cattle. Did you think of *that* when you appeared in juvenile court for him? I bet he was there tonight playing the god of power and the god of evil. Handing out death. And for what? For fifty dollars? For kicks? What about the cows? What about the calves?"

Dad continued to look at me without saying anything. I struggled for breath. "I let Edie out this morning. She's dead. You know that? She's dead. They hand-fed her poison. She walked up to them when they were lacing the salt block and they sprayed her mouth with poison. I heard them say so. They just killed her. Who's going to protect our cattle against this? We've got laws against child abuse and wife abuse. What about animal abuse? Who's going to protect the animals? They murdered my calf!"

I whipped around, picked a bowl off the end table and smashed it against the fireplace. The pieces flew into a mess on the floor. I could feel my shoulders heave and my stomach cramp. Dad reached over and enfolded me in his arms.

"I'm so sorry, honey. I'm so sorry about Edie," he said and rocked me gently. We stood there while I fought to get control of myself. My hands were shaking. I had never felt such a rage.

The phone rang. Sarah stood slowly and slipped over to the end table to answer it.

"It's Kevin." She offered the receiver to me.

I should have known he'd call. I was sending off enough energy to summon a Martian.

"Karen. Are you okay?"

"No. I'm not okay. I'm angry. I'm furious. Those bastards killed Edie." And then I started to cry great, heaving sobs.

"Holy shit, Karen." He swore. "Tell me."

So I told him. Between crying and sobbing and pacing around the room with the telephone on my ear, I told him. I saw Dad take his cellular phone and make a couple of calls. I guessed he was reporting the *Wipe Out* to the police. Sarah walked past me a couple of times as if she were afraid I was going to burst into flames.

I told Kevin about finding Edie, about the *Wipe Out*

and about Trevor and about the wickedness of it all. He listened. Gradually, I got some control over my feelings. They no longer seemed to be shooting up through my spine and off into the air, but were more contained within me, like rolling waves of anger. "And don't tell me she was just a cow!"

"I'm not going to. I feel like I lost a relative." His voice was deep and concerned.

I laughed a little at that and sniffed. Kevin had raised calves. He understood. "She was real, Karen. She had a real personality, an affectionate, stubborn, loving personality."

"Yes, she did." I sniffed again.

"She loved clover, remember? If you offered her a handful of grass she'd pick out the clover and eat it first."

"Yeah," I said. "She'd do that."

"Do you want me to come over?"

"No. It's all right. I'm okay. Better than I was." I needed him on the end of the telephone; he felt like part of myself, the accepting, calming part. But I didn't need him to come running over.

We talked for about forty minutes, and when I hung up I was less volatile. But I was still aware of a seething anger, not so uncontrollable now, but still there.

The doorbell rang. Dad answered it and brought Reena into the living room.

"Your dad called," she said. "You're upset by the poisoning. Phantom riders in the night. Organophosphates. Death."

"They killed my cow," I said flatly.

"Bastards," Reena said as she sat down. Dad poured coffee and set two mugs on the table.

"Sarah and I will watch TV in the den," he said. "You two can talk without us."

I looked at him and then at Reena. She nodded her thanks and pulled the coffee closer.

"Tell me about it," she said and waited.

I told her about it. This time I told the story with less passion, but I was still angry, vacillating between cold anger that solidified in my mind and the white heat of it that raged over my body. As I finished, the hot anger surged again. "It's wicked," I said. "They're twisted."

She nodded.

"How do you stand it when people deliberately do things like that to animals? When do you get so you can take that? So you don't care as much?"

"You can't be a vet if you don't care," she said. "At least, not a good one."

"That's it, then. I'm not going to be a vet. It kills me to see it."

"You'll get stronger."

"No." I shook my head. "I don't think so. I won't be able to do it. How do you stand it?"

"I cry," she said simply. "Every time." Her blue eyes seemed huge. I believed her. She did care and it did hurt her. I felt a little calmer.

"But how can you see the abuse and neglect and the deliberate killing like this and not die a little? Doesn't it take pieces out of you?"

"I'd care anyway," she said, "even if I wasn't a vet. As a vet, I can do something about some of it. I do what I can and I bleed for those I can't help."

I took a sip of the hot coffee and let it warm me. I wrapped my hands around the mug.

"I don't want that kind of hurt." I put my coffee mug down and hugged my elbows. I was cold.

Reena put her coffee cup down beside mine and faced me. "You think you can go through life without feeling? Without caring? Without hurting for something or somebody?"

I stared at her.

"Hurting is part of living, Karen. Caring is what makes the living beautiful. It comes in a package, the hurting with the caring."

"No." I dropped my head into my hands. "I don't want it. It hurts. It's horrible. I don't want to care." I thought about Kevin and his insistence that what we shared was important. If loving him meant this kind of hurt, I wasn't going to do it.

Reena stood suddenly and grabbed her truck keys. "Come with me."

I stood hesitantly. "Where are we going?"

"To my clinic." She called out our direction to Dad and headed for the back door. I followed her. It seemed easier to do as she said than to think of an alternative. Dad said he'd see me later and we left in Reena's truck.

She talked about her cases as we drove: about the calves on a ranch near town, about a horse who kept injuring himself breaking fences, about the clinic cat Willie, who lived in the back, about the goat in the outside pen and the calf in the corral.

When we got to the clinic, she unlocked the back door and took me into the central room, where the cages lined the walls. I felt a little numb, as if I couldn't think very clearly or very quickly. She began to introduce me to the animals in the clinic room.

"This is MacTavish," she said, moving toward a cage that contained a black and white dog. "He's a Border collie cross who jumped into the mower a month ago and sliced off one of his legs. A perky little troublemaker, he is, but happy and enthusiastic. I'll probably have to rescue him from disasters all his life."

We stopped in front of the cage and MacTavish sniffed our hands.

"He moves well on three legs. He's here this time as a boarder because his owner doesn't like to take him into the city when she vacations. MacTavish hates it here because he's lonesome, but he's also safe."

She moved to another cage. "This is Boots."

Boots was a golden cocker spaniel with an IV dripping into her front paw. Reena took some medication from the fridge, filled a syringe and added the medication to the IV line. I watched Boots, who looked unhappy.

"Boots, bless her, had not been eating well for several months before her owner brought her in. I couldn't find anything on the X-rays, so I finally did exploratory surgery. When I opened her up, I found a piece of linoleum and a bikini in her stomach."

I stared at Reena and then at the little dog. "A bikini? Reena, seriously?"

"True," she said. "Boots was a regular town dump. The bathing suit was causing quite a mess at the duodenal opening."

"You're kidding."

"No, really. It was stuck between the stomach and the intestines, and poor Boots was having trouble digesting anything, including the bikini. It was probably lycra or some other human-made fabric. Boots will feel a lot better tomorrow, won't you, darling?"

Boots looked woefully at us, lifted her head slightly, then plopped it back on her paws.

"Tomorrow," Reena promised.

Reena paused beside a cat cage. "This is Hortense. She came in with a lump on her back. Her owner thought I could just take it off, but being a conscientious owner she wanted me to check her over. And being a conscientious vet, I did. Hortense had three lumps, two more in the mammary glands, but they were all benign."

"Not cancerous?" I said, becoming a little interested in the fate of the cat.

"Right. I took them off and Hortense is going home tomorrow, perhaps getting more years of life because I re-moved what might one day have become cancerous. That was a satisfying surgery. I was fast and efficient," she said with some pride. "Hortense was lucky to have me." Reena ran her hand down Hortense's fur. The cat moved away. Reena laughed.

"Hortense is a little weird. She's afraid of everyone but her owner, so staying here is hard on her emotionally. Actually, Hortense is a little schizoid, but in cats that's acceptable. If the owner was willing to do nursing duty, I'd have sent Hortense home, but the owner is a little tense herself." Reena lifted her eyebrow and smiled as if to share the foibles of owners, but, at that moment, I did not share her fascination with the human race. She poured some water into the cat's dish and closed the cage door.

I was impatient. "Okay. I know you make a difference." If Reena brought me here to tell me that the life of a vet is a virtuous one, I knew that already. I just didn't think I could handle it.

"And," Reena said, walking toward the back room, "this is the freezer. In here I have the ones I didn't help."

The freezer was a shiny, white box big enough to hold a horse.

"It has corpses in it?" A freezer for dead animals?

She nodded and threw open the lid. Nothing stared back at me. There were only boxes and bags in there, no gruesome carcasses. Then I realized that the bags contained bodies.

Reena pointed at a lumpy, green, garbage bag. "This cat is going to the lab for study on something I couldn't diagnose. Maybe if they tell me what I missed, I'll help the next cat that presents the same symptoms. But this cat died. Fanny, her name was." She pointed to another lumpy bag, this one orange. "This is a poisoning, a dog that I didn't get in time. The owners are going to come in and take him away for burial at their place. Rupert, they called him."

She moved a little further down and touched a small

package. "This is a little girl's gerbil that she cried over — that we both cried over. I think the anesthetic killed Sammy. I have him in here so that I can do an autopsy on him and find out if there was anything wrong with his heart. If there isn't, I have to find out what I must do differently with the anesthetic on the next gerbil, but that won't help this little girl or her Sammy." She stepped back and slammed down the lid. "These are my mistakes."

I stared at the freezer. "How can you stand that?"

She shut off the light and walked toward the back door.

"The only way you keep from making mistakes in this world is to do nothing. The more you try, the more mistakes you make. It took a lot of heartache for me to understand that."

I was in the yard with her now, but I could still see the freezer in my mind, big, shiny, white and a constant reminder to Reena. I didn't want that.

"I want to be safe from mistakes and from all that hurting."

"There isn't any 'safe,'" she said.

I didn't want to believe her. "I don't have enough guts for this, Reena. The only way I can keep from hurting is not to care."

"True." Reena opened the door of her truck. "But not caring would make you a bad vet and a lousy human being."

She didn't say anything more on the drive home. I was quiet, thinking about the animals that she knew, the personalities, the emotions of the animals, the feelings in the air at the clinic. I thought about my own fury at the injustice and abuse animals had to endure. Somehow it all seemed part of the pattern of life that Reena lived, that maybe Dad lived, that other people understood and accepted as real, and not so much a crazy, impossible, unique problem that I had. Loving, caring, being open to the feelings of others, anger, hurt and affection were the best and the worst of being human.

Maybe rage against the mindless killing of animals was the best part of me. I leaned my head against the window of Reena's truck and let the tears come. I hated the poisoning.

Chapter 11

Ranch life was busy, so there wasn't much time to brood on Edie's death. I worked hard. When I thought of Edie I felt as if I were touching a bruise: tender, painful and always with me.

Kevin, his dad and brother had driven into their fall range-land to cut wood. He said he'd come to see me before he left for the coast, but we wouldn't have much time together. I tried not to think of either Edie or Kevin. I scheduled the mail delivery, cooking, Sarah's activities and ranch chores into a day that didn't leave time for depression.

The first day Trevor showed up for work, Dad and I had another argument.

"Where will Trevor be working?"

"I'm going to start him feeding the orphan calves and fencing the south line. You could bring the lunch out to the fence line and stay to work that line with him while I go to town for a couple of hours."

"Not in this lifetime."

He glanced at me from the corner of his eye. "Just bring us lunch then, all right? Or are you going to go on strike?"

"I'll bring the lunch." I didn't want to be around Trevor today, but Dad needed to eat.

At noon in the woods near the fence line, the day's plan changed.

"You're going to have to stay for a while, Karen," Dad told me as he ate. "I got a call from Lyle. The south fence is down."

I glared at him. He was brief.

"I have to help Lyle repair it, and it has to be now."

There wasn't any arguing with that.

"Just work on this section until I get back." Dad took my truck. His own had all the fencing supplies in it. I understood that Dad was not going back on our agreement. He *had* to respond to Mr. Jennings' phone call and fix the fence. He didn't see why Trevor should stand idly by while he did it. To keep Trevor working, I had to work with him. No one could pull wire and bang in staples at the same time — at least, not very easily. I knew all that, but I resented being left with Trevor. I didn't trust him, and I *knew* he had been poisoning our calves. *I* hadn't promised to supervise Trevor's community hours. I didn't want to be anywhere near him. Dad owed me big time.

There were four miles of fence to tighten and repair. I'd watched Dad and Trevor work when I first drove up, and I could see that Trevor knew how to use the fence stretchers. I threw the lunch papers and the thermos into the back of the truck, picked up my hammer and staples and headed for the wire.

"You ready, Trevor?"

"Yeah, I'm ready, but I have to be back at the barn by three to feed the calves."

"I'll drive you home then if Dad isn't back," I said curtly, and smacked the first staple in with a solid thunk. Trevor looked at me but said nothing as he kept the tension on the wire stretcher. I pounded the staples into the posts as Trevor held the wire taut, and we started working on the first mile of sagging barbed wire fence.

It was a hot afternoon. Trevor worked under the shade of the tall pines in his jeans, boots and gloves and without his shirt. He was as tall as Kevin and as broad shouldered, with dark, curly hair on his chest tapering to a V at his navel. I'd have had to be blind not to notice that. But he could look like a Calvin Klein model for all I cared; it wouldn't increase my heart rate. He'd tied a bandanna around his head to keep his hair out of his eyes, making him look like a pirate. Black Heart, he should be called. A man with the compassion of a toad.

We worked in silence for a few minutes and then Trevor said, "Are you taking chemistry this year, Karen?"

I looked at him and didn't answer, just banged in another staple.

"What's the matter with you?"

"Pull the wire tighter, Trevor." I waited while he put some muscle behind the stretchers and the wire was tight enough to pound in the next staple.

"What's the problem?" he persisted.

I banged the staples in one by one as I spoke. "The problem," *bang*, "is you fed my cow poison and killed her. She died screaming with pain. The problem," *bang*, "is you and your asshole friends are dripping poison like mindless demons. The problem," I said, as I banged in the rest of the staples, "is you are pond scum, a juvenile delinquent, a psychopath."

I let the hammer hang loosely in my hand and faced him. "I hope you and your *friends* waste out on drugs or alcohol and die in an overdose or drive yourself off a cliff!" I glared at him, letting him see the anger in my eyes. If he wanted to fight back, fine. I was ready. Maybe I was crazy to provoke him, but I didn't care. He had killed my calf and I hated him.

He stared at me and then looked away. His face flamed a bright red and he raised his hands and closed them into fists. "You've got a big mouth. Shut up, all right? Just shut up!"

I let the hammer drop and raised my hands in a karate blocking move. "Come on then, deadhead."

"Mouthy bitch!"

"Murderer!"

He jerked then, as if I'd hit him, slowly lowered his hands and stepped back. "Listen. You've got a father who cares and a family who's there for you. What do you know about making it on your own? You've got it good."

"My heart bleeds for you, Trevor. You poor little kid." Sarcasm dripped from my tongue. "So you kill animals and threaten little kids to make yourself feel loved? Tell me another story."

He looked at me quickly, then stared at the ground. "I'm sorry about your sister. That was a mistake. I got carried away."

I let my hands fall. Sarah hadn't been afraid of him at the 4-H sale, but I'd been furious and scared.

He glanced at me again and then studied the fence stretchers, hanging from the wire where he'd left them. "Let's just drop it, okay?"

I nodded, my anger gone for the moment. It had flared in an instant, fierce and overwhelming. But it was gone now. I didn't know if I had always been a person who had fierce emotions like this or if I was only now understanding how deep and strong they were, but I hardly knew myself.

"Look, Karen," Trevor said evenly. "Chill out, okay? I don't want to be here. But either I work for your dad or I go to a detention home. There aren't any second chances for me. I have to do this."

I shrugged. "Do I care? No. A detention home would be a good place for you. Jail would be better."

He took a deep breath and let it out slowly. Then he half closed his eyes and smiled a condescending smile, as if I were a child he was humouring. I remembered Mary Jane telling me once that when you lose your temper, you give away power. I had a hint of what she meant then. I was the one who felt frustrated. Trevor didn't understand any better about the deaths of the calves than he had before I lost my temper. That just made me more angry.

I almost hoped he'd start something, but he walked to the next section of fence. I picked up more staples and followed him.

He fitted the stretchers on the wire, then turned to me. "Okay. Let's do it this way. I'll work here, but you don't have to get along with me. You don't even have to talk to me."

"Great. Suits me. Pull that wire."

He reached for the next wire, fitted the fence stretchers on it and pulled. I stapled it down. We worked together without saying another word for two hours.

Telling Trevor off then pounding staples felt good. Maybe I should have been afraid of him, isolated as we were. But somehow here, on my own ranch, in my own woods, I felt safe. That didn't mean that I *was* safe, just that I *felt* safe. A soft breeze stirred the pine boughs overhead and sent the smell of pitch through the warm summer afternoon. A Swainson's thrush dropped its clear, bell tones from high in the air. It was the best of the summer, peaceful, warm and quiet. If Trevor had made one threatening move on me, I would have hit him with the hammer.

Dad returned and I drove back to the house.

I saw Trevor occasionally after that, when he arrived in the morning and sometimes at lunch. He said very little to me and seemed to be trying to be nice to Sarah. After he had been working on the ranch a few days, I adjusted slowly to the idea of community service. Maybe Dad *could* influence him; he sure kept him busy. Trevor had to bottle-feed three orphan calves every four hours, help with the fencing and shovel out the barn and the chicken house. Maybe community service would make a difference to him.

I spent some of my time choosing another cow from Dad's herd to replace Edie. I studied the computer records and drove out into the pastures, checking the cows, trying to make sure I was choosing the conformation I wanted. Dad would charge me market price when I bought from him, but I should get that back on my first calf sale.

I didn't have any reason to work with Trevor again until a few days later. Dad was expecting a forestry inspector to check some trees on Crown land. He asked me to drive the inspector to the fence line when he arrived.

"Lend me your truck, Karen," he said when I arrived at the fence line with the tall, thin, quiet government man. "You finish this fencing with Trevor, will you? I need to show the inspector which trees are threatening to fall onto the south fence." We needed permission to cut Crown timber.

There wasn't really any choice. Dad's truck was full of fencing equipment. I slid from my truck, grabbed my hammer from the box and walked toward the fence — and Trevor.

"Pack up and drive my truck home by three," Dad yelled at me as he left.

I nodded. Trevor said nothing. I said nothing, just picked up some staples and started working. We worked for two hours saying little but "Pull it tighter" or "Hand me more staples."

A cow and calf wandered past us once, the calf curious about everything. We stopped working to watch him. He walked closer, awkwardly lurching over the brush and uneven ground until he was only a few feet away, where he stopped and stared at us. We stared back. Then he suddenly turned and dashed to his momma, all gangling legs and long tail. We laughed. For a moment I forgot who Trevor was and what he had done.

Just before three we finished the job. "We'll go back now. All the tools have to come in with us — " I remembered then that this was Trevor — "because we have these marauding idiots on bikes who pick up anything that isn't nailed down."

Trevor looked at me but said nothing, just picked up the tools and dropped them into the box of the truck.

I stopped by the house. "You know where the milk bottles are, don't you?"

He nodded. Dad had been allowing him to fetch them at feeding time.

Trevor walked toward the house and the fridge on the back porch. I took my hammer into the barn. It was my personal hammer, and I wanted to put it back in my tool box.

The calves got to their feet and ambled to the board fence as I walked past their pen. When Trevor arrived with the bottles, they jostled each other and tried to reach over the top of the railing.

"Hey," he said. "Take it easy." Sarah had fed the calves for the first four weeks, but they were too big for her now and knocked her over when she got near them.

I stopped to watch. "They know you're the one with the food."

"You think they do?" He seemed surprised.

"Sure they do. I walked in and they weren't interested in me; you walk in and they're excited."

He turned back to the calves. He had a big pop bottle with a large nipple on it in the mouth of one calf, and the same in the mouth of another. Both were sucking greedily and quickly. The third calf was mooing and complaining.

"I've only got two hands, buddy."

"Do you want me to feed that one?" I asked.

"Uh, no. Thanks. That's Goofy. He has a problem with his tongue, so you have to hold his head when he eats. I like to feed him last because he takes longer."

I glanced at Trevor. Sarah hadn't told me about this calf, or maybe she had and I hadn't heard her. "What's the matter with his tongue?"

Trevor took the empty bottle away from one calf and waited for a moment while the second calf finished. Then he picked up the remaining full bottle and climbed the fence, moving the calves aside until he was close to the third one. He put his arm around the calf and held its head still while slipping the bottle inside its mouth. After a couple of shakes of its head, the calf started to drink. Trevor paid close attention and seemed to move his hands in a kind of dance with the calf's head, making sure the bottle stayed in the mouth.

"Your dad says that Goofy here has some kind of nerve damage so his tongue doesn't work quite right, but he thinks it will get better."

"Oh?" I hadn't seen that before in a calf and I was interested. "Won't that keep it from pulling on grass and feeding itself when it's older?" Cattle need their tongues to feed themselves. A damaged tongue might mean starvation.

"Dan thinks it will get better. I've only been feeding him for a few days, but I think it *is* getting better."

We watched the calf together and I realized that Trevor and I had spoken without anger.

"Do you have pets at home, Trevor?" I asked curiously. He was careful with Goofy and successful at getting the milk into him.

"No," he said. "My dad's got asthma and he's allergic to animals."

Maybe I should have felt a little sorry for him. I couldn't imagine not having animals around me. The other two calves were crowding Trevor, but he was big enough and strong enough to keep them away while he fed Goofy.

"Sarah told me she named these calves," Trevor said.

"Yeah."

"What did she call them?"

"Candy and Floss."

Trevor winced and shook his head. "Candy and Floss? For calves?"

"Hey, be grateful. She was going to call them Dental

and Floss."

He laughed. I left him then and went back to my own work.

For the next week I managed to see Trevor at lunch, work with him occasionally and watch him feed the calves without losing my temper. Dad told me he was pleased to see I had a "mature reticence." I didn't tell him about blasting Trevor in the woods that first day. I had to admit to Dad that Trevor gradually became a good worker. He completed the chores Dad assigned him and was even able to work on his own some of the time.

"He's never had anything to do that mattered before," Dad told me. "No one gave him real work."

I didn't know if it was that, or the fact that Dad is a good boss, but Trevor managed the work.

The biggest surprise was the way he enjoyed feeding the calves. He spent more time than Dad expected, feeding them, petting them and cleaning their stalls. He talked to them all the time as well, particularly Goofy. He even spent time massaging Goofy's jaw, hoping it would help heal the nerve damage. He swore that Goofy was much better, but I didn't see it myself.

There was one more week of summer vacation left. Trevor was going to work with us on the ranch for that week and then for six weekends after that. Kevin would leave for college when he returned from the bush. Mom was supposed to be home just after school started. I hoped she would make it because I didn't think I could deal with Sarah's school and after-school activities. I couldn't get her on the school bus and to all those lessons — dancing, music, Brownies and 4-H — and listen to her talk about everything that went on in her day, and complain about most of it. It all took so much time.

"It's a privilege," Sarah told me at breakfast. "Most people would be glad to have a kid who wanted to do all that."

I looked at her wonderingly. "Is that what Mom told you?"

"Yes," she said smugly.

"And you believed her?"

She blinked, but was only stopped for a moment. "You're just jealous," she said.

Dad and Trevor were a little late coming in at noon because they had led the calves out into the pasture. Perhaps Goofy might have trouble trying to eat grass, but he would come back to the barn at night on his own to get a bucket of milk. I was worried about them, but Dad said they had to get on the grass soon or they wouldn't grow properly; we couldn't keep them penned up forever. I wondered how Trevor would feel about letting them out, whether he'd be like Paula and hate to part with them. But if he felt anything, he didn't mention it when he came in.

Constable Fraser pulled in with his squad car just after Dad and Trevor arrived for lunch. Lunch was a do-it-your-self-affair, so Fraser joined the line and made a couple of sandwiches for himself. Trevor sat at the end of the table as far away from the constable as possible. Sarah, as usual, acted as though Will Fraser had come to see her and chatted to him all through lunch.

"Did you get anywhere on finding out who's killing our cattle?" I asked him when Sarah finally wound down.

"Not a lot," he said. "We've checked into all the stores that sell *Wipe Out*. There hasn't been much sold and no one can remember selling to anyone who wouldn't have a good reason for it."

"So," I said, "only ranchers with cattle who would need it as a worm medication bought it?"

"That's right."

"Ranchers wouldn't poison other ranchers' cattle," Dad said. "At least, you wouldn't think so."

"Well, you wouldn't think so," Will agreed, "but we

aren't ruling it out."

Trevor said nothing.

I looked at Dad. He lowered his eyebrows and shot me a warning stare. Don't blame Trevor. I could hear him say it as clearly as if he'd spoken aloud. I kept my mouth closed, but I still thought it. Trevor was behind the poisonings.

Dad pushed his chair back. "Nice to see you, Will. Stay as long as you want, but I've got to get back to the fencing. I'd like to get them all tight before the snow flies."

"I understand it's a race," Will said. "Six weeks before the snow comes and ten miles of fence?"

"Something like that," Dad said. "You coming, Trevor?" That was Dad's polite way of saying, "Get moving, Trevor."

"I'd like to keep Trevor for a few minutes," Will said, leaning back in his chair. "I have some questions for him."

"Okay." Dad looked over at me. "Karen. Drive Trevor to the mill site when he's finished here, would you? I'll be working there. Bring your gloves, Trevor."

Trevor nodded.

I rose. "Come on, Sarah. You can help me with the laundry."

Sarah made a face. I raised my eyebrows and, for once, she understood.

"Bang on the floor when you're ready, Trevor," I said, and headed downstairs with Sarah following me.

"You wanted to leave them alone because Trevor has to talk to the police about his court stuff. Is that right, Karen?"

I stopped at the door of laundry room. "Way to go, Squirt. You get 'A' for comprehension. That's exactly what I wanted you to do."

"I knew that."

She was so pleased with herself that she helped me fold clothes without complaint until Trevor called me.

"Just finish this pile and take them to the bedrooms, okay Sarah?"

She agreed to do that. I didn't think this cooperation would last long, but it was a nice change from her usual arguments.

Trevor picked up his fencing gloves from the counter on the porch and followed me to my truck. He slammed the door and I started the engine.

"So, did you help the constable get the answers to his questions?"

Trevor shot a look out of the corner of his eye, then shrugged. "I don't know a thing."

He wouldn't betray his friends. His idea of right and wrong stunk. He was loyal to creeps who killed cows. We didn't speak as I drove down the road toward the mill site, curved around the lake and crossed the meadow where I'd seen the bikers last week.

"Hey," Trevor said suddenly. "There's a calf down."

I slammed on the brakes. "Where?"

"Over there, by the hay shed."

My eyes swept the meadow until I saw the brown hump in the grass. I put the truck into low gear, drove to the shed, cut the engine and jumped out. I knelt in front of the stricken calf.

It was alive, but twitching. Trevor came around from the other side of the truck and squatted down beside me. "What's the matter?"

"It looks like that poison spray, *Wipe Out*. It's an organophosphate and it causes convulsions and death. You ought to know all about it."

"Karen," Trevor said. His voice sounded high. "It's Goofy."

I looked hard at the calf for a moment. "Yeah," I said. "It is."

Trevor shot to his feet. "Don't just sit there," he said, almost yelling at me. "*Do* something."

I sprinted to the passenger side of the truck and pulled a syringe and the Atropine from the glove compartment. I had given shots to cattle since I was Sarah's age, but this one had to go into the jugular vein. Dad had shown me how to do it. I had the theory.

"Karen," Trevor yelled again. "He's jerking and crying."

The calf screamed.

Do one thing at a time, I said to myself. Ignore everything else right now; get the medicine. I broke open the package and stuck the needle into the bottle. The dose was written on the package. I pulled out the correct amount and ran back to the calf.

The calf was in a full seizure, thrashing and jerking. I waited for a second until it was still, then felt along its neck for the rope-like vein that ran up the outside. I pushed the needle in, drew back on the plunger to make sure I was in the vein and not a muscle and then pushed the medication in.

"Will it really help?" Trevor demanded.

"Reena said it's the only thing that works. If it doesn't make a difference the first time, I'm supposed to do it again in five minutes. But if it doesn't work the first time, she said, it usually doesn't work at all."

"It better work." Trevor had his hand on Goofy's shoulder and was patting it. "It's going to work, Goof, sure it is. Just hold on there."

The calf looked at Trevor and feebly tried to nuzzle his hand. Trevor's eyes teared and he fondled the calf's ears. "You'll be all right, Goofy. Karen's got this medicine for you. You'll be all right."

I held the bottle of Atropine in my left hand and the syringe in my right and waited. A loon on the bay warbled a crazy cry. A killdeer dived over us and then flew toward the hay shed. I watched the calf. For a minute I thought we'd won. Then the tremors started again, increasing in severity until the calf rolled his eyes back and shuddered. I withdrew another dosage and plunged it into his neck, but

I could see that he had stopped breathing. I squatted back on my heels and just looked at him.

"What's the matter?" Trevor said.

"He's dead."

"No. He's not dead. Give him another shot."

"He's dead, Trevor."

"Don't just stand there. *Do* something!" Trevor grabbed my shoulder and shook me.

I broke his hold as I stood quickly. "Roll him on his back."

Trevor pulled Goofy's feet up and turned him a little. I knelt over the calf and slammed my fist into his chest wall where I thought his heart was and then checked for some signs of life. Nothing.

"Let him go, Trevor," I said.

Trevor let the calf's feet drop and watched as its weight pulled it to its side. He stared at the calf and let his hand move slowly over its head. The calf's eyes stared at nothing, its tongue lolled out of its mouth, saliva dripped onto the ground. Trevor patted its head and ran his hand over its shoulder.

"Goofy?" he said. "Son of a bitch. Goofy?" I left him with the calf and walked around the meadow, searching the ground. I found the can of *Wipe Out* near the hay shed, underneath a loose board. There must have been two cans of poison here the night Edie died. I had missed this one when I had searched the meadow, and Goofy had found it. Calves always get into the crannies and the corners. They're curious, I suppose. I picked up the can carefully and pitched it into the box of the truck.

"What's that?" Trevor said as he straightened.

"Poison," I said. "*Wipe Out.*"

Trevor crossed his arms and stood rigidly looking out over the lake. He took a couple of deep breaths. I waited.

I was sorry that Goofy had died and I hated to see him

die in convulsions, but, in spite of what Dad told Trevor, I didn't think he would have been able to eat well with his damaged tongue. I put the Atropine back in the glove compartment. My white fury about the poisoning had gone into the air the night Edie died. Now I felt a cold anger. How many calves would die, I wondered?

Trevor was still staring at the lake. I went over to him and touched his arm. He turned to me and his eyes were full of tears. "Karen, he liked me. That Goofy really liked me."

I nodded. It was true. Trevor and Goofy had been friends, but, unless I was totally wrong, it was Trevor who had killed him. "He trusted you too."

Trevor looked as though I'd hit him. Good. I wanted him to hurt. Really hurt. Calves had died because of him. He should understand what that meant. He should *feel* what that meant. It wasn't enough to understand with your mind, you had to accept the feelings. That suddenly seemed very important to me. You had to accept the feelings. Trust them. Act on them. Trevor's eyes reflected pain before he squeezed them shut.

"Oh God," he said. "This isn't happening. I can't *care* this much about a calf."

"Why not?" I said. "Goofy was real. He had a personality, feelings, likes and dislikes. He knew who you were. He relied on you. No wonder you cared about him. He cared about you too."

If Trevor had been almost anyone else, I would have tried to comfort him, not increase the pain, but he had caused this with his stupid, careless, criminal behaviour. He could feel it the way I felt it. I wanted him to suffer.

Chapter 12

I left Trevor with the dead calf and drove up the trail to the mill site, looking for Dad. I found him standing under some pine trees, struggling with wire. It looped around his arms and spilled down onto the ground beyond the sagging section of fence. When I told him about Goofy, he threw his tools into his truck and followed me back to the meadow. Trevor was kneeling beside the dead calf. By the time I'd killed my engine, Dad was standing with his hand on Trevor's shoulder.

"Sorry, Trev. Sometimes they don't make it."

Trevor nodded. His cheeks were wet; his hand still cradled the calf's head. He kept his eyes down.

"We kind of got to know each other," he said. "He was a neat calf."

"You treated him okay. He liked you." Dad patted Trevor on the shoulder again. Trevor glanced at him for a second and then turned back to the calf. Dad and I stood quietly.

"Okay then." Dad broke the silence. "Let's get this calf in the back of my truck. We can use the come-along and winch it in." Dad attached the cable to the calf and we winched it slowly to the edge of the truck box. I kept my fingers on the on-off switch of the motor that operated the winch while Dad and Trevor pulled and shoved until Goofy was resting on the deck. When Dad signalled, I flipped the switch off. The silence was deep and heavy. I joined Dad and Trevor at the truck box and we stared at the calf.

"Do you know anything about this, Trevor?" Dad asked quietly.

Trevor continued to look intently at Goofy.

"Trevor?" Dad insisted.

"Yeah." Trevor still didn't look at either of us.

"Suppose you tell me."

The wind rustled the leaves of the poplar tree at the lake's edge. A loon ran across the water in a clumsy launch into the air. The lake looked calm.

Trevor sighed. "I'll tell you."

The hair on my arms prickled and I suddenly felt cold. I had been right. Trevor was guilty, but for a second, I couldn't believe it.

"So." Dad took a deep breath. "Go ahead."

"Bryan Tyeson wants your land," Trevor said, his eyes darting to Dad's face and then away.

"Bryan Tyeson?" Dad was incredulous. "The bank manager? That Tyeson?"

Trevor kept his eyes averted and spoke in jerky sentences, his voice controlled and flat.

"Yeah. He's bought up everything to the north of you. He's got a company ready to develop it if he can get your property to tie the whole section to the lake. It's a package deal. No lakeside property, no deal. My dad told me that. Tyeson didn't say anything about it. Tyeson thinks I'm stupid."

Trevor didn't look at Dad or me, but gazed over the lake, his hands clenched at his sides, his body rigid. "I think he wants to force you to sell. Maybe he figures dying cattle would make you want quick money."

The breeze stirred my hair and blew a few strands across my face. I tucked it behind my ears absently. Andy Foster made sense. Tyeson didn't make sense.

Dad leaned on his hands on the edge of the truck box. "Why did you do it?" The poison. Dad was asking Trevor about the poison.

"Money." Trevor still couldn't look at us. His voice continued in that flat monotone. "I got paid. Tyeson gave each of us fifty bucks a night. My dad's always talking about making money. I figured I could make some on my own. Fifty bucks a night is good money. And then there was the park. My dad wants to make this lake property a private park. A park would make real estate go up out this way if people could use the lake. And me and my friends could use the sawdust pit for dirt biking. I figured I could make money and have some fun . . . ." His voice died away. Neither Dad nor I spoke and, after a second, Trevor continued. "And Dad would make money too."

Money again. What kind of a man was Andy Foster? Had he told Trevor to do this? Even if he had, even if he wasn't a great role model or the kind of father I'd want, his son wasn't a child. Trevor made his own decisions, and they had included spreading poison.

Dad reached out and gripped Trevor's shoulder. Trevor had to look at him. "Is your Dad in on this then?"

"No," Trevor said quickly. Now he looked straight at Dad. "No, he didn't know about Tyeson's having the cattle poisoned. I just figured it fit in pretty good with what he wanted to do. My dad doesn't know."

Dad pursued it. "Your dad must know that Tyeson is the principal in the company that's buying the land."

Trevor nodded. Dad continued.

"And he must know that Tyeson should *not* be the principal."

"It's not illegal," Trevor said. "At least, Dad says it's not illegal."

"Not exactly illegal. A little irregular, though. The bank supervisors wouldn't like it."

Trevor insisted his dad was just conducting real estate business with Tyeson, not placing poison on the land. Was Trevor protecting his Dad or telling the truth?

"Tyeson." Dad shook his head. "He's a bank manager. He's not supposed to be making money on the side on property deals, especially not if he's using inside information about his clients' financial affairs."

"Yeah?" Trevor said. "Well, he probably shoves the rules around to make room for himself. It was a pretty good plan, you know. People were starting to sell. A couple, anyway."

I leaned on the edge of the truck box and looked down at Goofy. Dad crossed his arms and stood back. Trevor turned and looked at the calf. His hand drifted over the side of the truck and down onto Goofy's head. He fondled Goofy's ears and petted his head.

A loon cried again, a long, raucous, wild cry of possession. We were in his bay. I thought of Tyeson, who wanted this bay, and Dad, who had title to it. Who should own it? It was our home. It belonged to the loon as well. Tyeson wanted it so he could turn it into a private beach where hundreds of people could use it — and so he could make money. Conflicting uses. Still, none of us had the right to kill for it. Tyeson was willing to cause all this pain so he could make money. What kind of a man was he? Friendly, cheerful and sophisticated? Cruel, selfish and wicked? The man who was going to see that I got a scholarship? Bryan Tyeson's character traits chased themselves around my head.

"Back! Back!" Without warning, Dad exploded in anger. "Back to the house. I'm calling Will Fraser."

Trevor jerked his hand away from Goofy and glanced at Dad. "I guess," he said.

Will didn't get to the house for a couple of hours. Dad dug a pit with the backhoe and buried Goofy deep in the ground. He didn't want any poison working its way into the grass.

"I'm not sure it can," he said, "but poison has a way of cycling around from one source to another."

Trevor had said very little since we had returned to the house. He helped Dad with Goofy, but spent the rest of the time in the kitchen, staring through the windows at the lake, waiting. Dad and I left him alone. Dad needed time to let his temper cool, and I didn't think I'd ever speak to Trevor again. Yet the hate I'd felt for him earlier wasn't as strong now. He had really cared about Goofy, cared so much that he put himself in jeopardy. That made it harder to hate him, but I left him alone. Dad stared out the window, and Trevor was so deep in his own thoughts he didn't even see us. When Will finally came, the tension in the air was as thick as fog.

Dad met Will at the door, told him about the poisoning and then invited him to the table. I pulled a chair close. I could hear muted sounds from the television in the basement recreation room where Sarah was enthralled with a video. A Steller's jay squawked outside the window and then disappeared in a flash of blue. Inside, we waited.

"Trevor has something to say," Dad finally offered.

Trevor took a deep breath and started. He told Will about Bryan Tyeson, repeated what he'd said about his dad being innocent and admitted to spraying the poison.

Will sat back with his arms crossed and said little except, "And then?" "What did he hope to gain?" "How often did you do that?" and "When did he pay you?"

Trevor was heading for the detention home for sure with his answers, but he didn't seem to care. Will cautioned him once with the you-have-the-right-to-remain-silent clause, but Trevor didn't stop talking.

"Why did you decide to tell us now?" Fraser said.

"The calf that died today," Trevor said. "He was . . . ."

"Trevor's friend," I said.

Trevor bit his bottom lip, but continued. "There are still calves out there."

Candy and Floss were out there. Those must be the calves Trevor meant; he hadn't worried about Edie.

Dad got the coffee. I got the cream and sugar. We settled back. There hadn't been a sound since Trevor stopped talking. Will Fraser nodded his thanks to both of us, then gave Trevor a level look.

"You're in trouble, Trevor."

Trevor shrugged and looked over the lake. Dad ignored Trevor and studied his coffee cup, turning it round and round in his hands. Finally, he looked at Will Fraser.

"There's got to be some reason why Tyeson's so desperate to get this land. Why wouldn't he wait for another piece to come on the market, or try another lake?"

"Time limits create pressure," Fraser said. "Maybe he's running out of time."

"To flip the property? To create money?"

Fraser nodded.

"What kind of pressure would it take?"

"Drug debts." Fraser shot a look at Trevor. "Is Tyeson dealing or using drugs?"

Trevor shook his head. "I don't know. I don't think so."

"Bad investments. Fraud. Embezzlement at the bank. I'll put a check on his bank accounts and see if I can find a pattern of big payments or big debts and big payoffs."

"Where would he get the money to buy?" Dad asked.

Trevor looked up.

"Yes?" Dad said. "You've thought of something?"

"He said once that he was lucky in the casino. Maybe he won the money."

"You don't win if you gamble much." Will stood suddenly and paced back and forth in the kitchen. A frown of concentration wrinkled his forehead, as if he were searching his mind for information. He cracked the knuckles of his fingers as he paced. "More likely," he said, "he lost enough to make him vulnerable to a gambling company. He's probably fronting for them. They need legitimate deals to move money around. I'll look into that." He spoke more quickly now. "I didn't know he was a gambler. If he's addicted, he'd be an easy mark for crime organizations, because he wouldn't be able to stop."

I thought about this. They went together: gambling, crime, money, greed.

Dad nodded. "Addictive gambling would keep him from feeling anything. It would deaden his conscience."

Will agreed, then said briskly as he sat down, "Tyeson may owe the company money. They might suggest he buy some land for them in the Cariboo. He buys the land in his name. When he sells it, the profits go to the casino company or, more likely, to a company that lends money to casino patrons. Then Tyeson loses again to the casino and they finance him again and that way they keep the man making money for them while he loses it for himself. It's a common pattern, more common than most people believe. That's a good lead, Trevor. It might fit. I'll follow it up."

Dad frowned. "I don't understand why he thinks that poisoning cattle will force me to sell. I've told him that I won't sell, that losing cattle won't force me out."

Trevor stared at his coffee cup for a moment. "I asked him why we were doing it. At first he said you'd sell if enough cows died. When he knew you wouldn't, he said he'd just kill the cattle to keep you worried."

"It didn't bother him," Dad said slowly, "that the calves died?"

"He didn't think about it, I guess. *We* didn't think about it. It was like it was just a game, like we were going to win."

"So," Dad said, "is he trying to keep me dealing with crisis here while he looks for a way to force me to sell?"

"I don't know," Trevor said. "Maybe. He's acting nervous. Talks fast about 'controlling the market,' and 'playing for high stakes.' Sometimes shouts at us. He used to be quieter. I don't know. He's different. He might keep harassing you, and he might just stop."

"Pressure's building up on him maybe," Will said.

I looked out the window at the lake, not really seeing it. What would a desperate man do? I thought about his visit to us here at the house, and turned over in my mind the conversation we'd had. "When he was here — remember, Dad? — we talked about the poison. You told him it wouldn't slow us down. You told him the only thing that would slow us down would be losing our hay and that we had it all under cover."

"Where is your hay?" Fraser asked.

Dad and I looked at each other. An alarm reverberated through my brain. "Fire," we breathed the words at the same time.

Dad explained it to Will. "If Tyeson burns our hay, we'd be in financial trouble. He knows that. The worst financial blow he could strike would be setting our hay piles on fire."

Fraser rubbed his forehead. "Man, we don't have the staff to guard your hay. You're going to have to do that yourself."

Dad turned to Trevor. "Could he be planning to torch our hay piles?"

Trevor was quiet for a moment. "Maybe," he said slowly. "He said something about a quicker way, a . . . ." He looked puzzled. "A noninsured way?"

"Right," Dad said. "I don't have insurance on the hay. I can't get insurance on the hay. Tyeson knows that. The bank asks about it. It's called noninsurable, noncreditable inventory. They won't lend money on hay. Burning our hay piles would be a quick and easy thing to do."

Dad leaned toward Trevor. "We need to know when Tyeson's going to move on us. Could you help?"

Trevor eyed Dad cautiously. "Maybe."

"Keep your eyes open," Dad said. "Let us know if Tyeson does anything suspicious."

"I might not see him. I mean, I don't see him that

much. I might not *know*!"

"You might not, but if you do notice anything, call us."

Trevor swallowed. "Okay."

"Good man."

I felt sick. They treated this new threat like the game Trevor was talking about, as if the next move was Tyeson's and they were going to block it. I could think of a hundred things that might go wrong. Trevor could warn Tyeson. Trevor could have been lying through his teeth right now and report everything to Tyeson. It seemed to me that Trevor wanted to please his friends, Tyeson and his Dad. Now he'd said he wanted to please my Dad and Fraser. Why trust him? As well, I had a hard time picturing Bryan Tyeson, tall, friendly, normal looking, being so compelled to gamble that he'd sneak through the woods and torch our shed. And Dad's relying on Trevor seemed to me to be downright silly.

Will Fraser pulled away in his squad car and Trevor rode home on his bike. Dad drove out to the hay shed by the lake and left a pump with a hose connected and set up on the lakeside. "I don't think Tyeson will drive up here in the daylight," he said, "but I left Pinto on guard there. I'll check back a couple of times in the night."

There wasn't much else we could do. Dad said he might as well give up on ranch work for the day and why didn't we get busy cleaning the house before Mom came home? Sarah protested until Dad put her in charge of organizing the chores — a brilliant idea. When she is in charge, Sarah divides the work fairly. I got the oven, which wasn't too bad because it has an automatic cleaning system; she got the bathrooms; and Dad got the vacuuming. We worked together for two hours, about my limit on housework, and managed to get a lot done.

"Pretty good," Dad said as we surveyed the house when we had finished. It did look better.

"How about dinner in front of the living room television?" Sarah was still organizing us. "Fridge pick-ups?"

Dad and I agreed, so we scavenged through the refrigerator, made our own meals, took them to the living room and watched Sarah's video, *Black Beauty*. She was happy to see it again and Dad and I enjoyed it. Dad checked on the hay shed and Pinto at ten, and all was well. *Black Beauty* didn't bother me the way horror shows did, so sleep came minutes after I fell into bed.

It was one in the morning when the telephone rang. I answered it.

"Karen," Trevor said, his voice soft as if he were trying to keep from being heard. Rock music and voices rose and fell in the background. "Tell your dad. Tyeson's bought a jerry can of gas."

"When?"

"Tonight, about eleven."

"It took you two hours to decide to phone us?" I didn't believe him.

"I didn't see him. One of my friends did. I just heard about it now. Tell your dad."

Chapter 13

Dad talked to Trevor, then phoned the police. I dressed quickly and called Jock. Dad lifted Sarah from her bed, blankets and all, and deposited her on the living room couch.

"Jock will stay with you, Sarah. Mrs. Jennings will be over soon." The dog dropped to the floor near Sarah's head. She nodded her sleepy understanding; she would be alone in the house. I tumbled into Dad's truck, slammed the door and snapped on my seat belt as Dad tore out of the yard.

"Where will we meet the police?"

"At the hay shed. I'm not going to waste time guiding them through the woods. I told them to pick up Trevor. He can lead them in. I asked Trevor; he said he'd do it."

"Dad, if Bryan Tyeson is desperate . . . ."

"Yeah?"

"If he's desperate, won't he be dangerous?"

"No. He's a banker. He's used to pens and pencils and computers. He'll be scared to death out in the woods at night and he'll be afraid to face us. He'll probably drop the gas and cry."

I hoped Dad was right.

"What equipment do we have?"

"A hose, a pump at the lake and two fire extinguishers in the back of the truck."

The hose would be in the lake, attached to a pump on the shore. Dad would turn on the pump's gas engine. The engine would suck water from the lake and force the water through the hose on the other side of the pump with enough pressure to reach the top of the hay pile. The fire extinguishers would spray only a short distance.

We tore over the dirt road, banging into potholes and skidding around corners. We burst through the woods at the edge of the meadow to find everything quiet. Pinto rose from his guard position at the front of the hay pile and trotted over to the truck.

"In," Dad commanded Pinto. The dog hopped onto the floor of the cab.

"Where are we going?"

"Up to the mill site to wait there for the police or Tyeson . . . whoever comes first."

The police arrived just as we drove into the site, Will Fraser and a policewoman I didn't know in the first car, with Trevor in the back seat, and two more policemen in the second. Will leaned out his window. "We'll stake out the hay shed, Dan. There'll be five of us, so we should get him."

"Six," Dad said. "Karen can operate the hose if you guys get tied up with the prisoner."

Will looked at me. "I don't know, Dan. I don't want too many civilians out there. It could get confusing, and I might lose track of where everyone is."

"Karen's coming." The problem of arson was Dad's, on his ranch; he was going to stay in charge of it. "You guys want Tyeson; I want my hay."

"All right," Will agreed reluctantly. "Stay in the trees until Tyeson arrives. I want Tyeson with a match in his hand before I charge him with arson."

"No way," Dad said emphatically. "He's not torching my hay. He can pour the gas, but I'm stopping him before he puts a flame to it. That's as much cooperation as you'll get from me. Nothing more."

Will argued. "I'd like to make the charge stick, Dan. If we stop him from lighting the fire tonight, he could evade conviction. He'll tell us that he was only looking for something he dropped, or he had gas with him to kill mice, or some crazy reason that at least two lawyers in this town would persuade a jury was 'reasonable doubt of guilt.'"

He was right. Tyeson might talk his way out of the charge.

Dad would not budge. "You heard it. That's my winter hay we're talking about. Besides, he could set the woods on fire."

Will gave up. "All right."

Once we had an understanding, the police drove their cars into the cover of the trees and walked with us to the meadow.

The large circular meadow was beautiful in the moonlight — calm, quiet and peaceful. I had been here often, but tonight everything looked bigger and more dramatic. The hay shed loomed over us, the two-storey-tall log poles supporting the shiny aluminum roof. Just beyond the hay shed, the lake stretched like a shadow into the shimmering path of moonlight. Fir trees and willow bushes rose in a ragged fringe along the shore. A tractor trail led into the meadow from the trees and continued in two dark wheel tracks to the hay shed.

Will stationed the constables at four equal points of a circle around the open area of the meadow and told Dad and me to stay by the big tree near the pump. We carried both fire extinguishers with us, dropped them at the bottom of the fir tree and turned our backs to the lake. The tractor trail emerged from the trees on our right, passed in front of us and continued on a short distance to the hay shed. If Tyeson drove this trail, we were in a perfect position to see him.

Trevor slipped in beside Dad. "I can help," Trevor said quietly. "I *need* to help."

Dad turned his head and looked at him. "Stay with me

then," he said, "and do what I tell you."

"Thanks," Trevor breathed.

We sat on the ground and leaned against the tree. At first there was no sound at all; then I heard the lapping of the water on the lakeshore as the breeze created small waves; then the rustle of the wind in the willow bushes like the whisper of tissue paper, delicate and momentary; then the loon announcing to anyone who could hear that we were invading his bay again. His wild cries echoed off the far shore and bounced back to us — crazy laughing, Sarah calls it — warning us in peals of manic cries that this was his territory. An owl in the trees behind us sent a drumming question into the night air about who these strangers in his woods were. His resonant bass tone skipped over the meadow in the air and hung there until another owl, far off across the bay and high in a fir, answered with its own question.

I was tense, but tried to will a calm feeling into my body in case Kevin was picking up my mood. I didn't need him worrying about me. The wind died. The night was still. We waited.

After an hour, when my hands were cold and I was seriously wondering if Trevor had told us the truth, headlights flashed for a second on the old mill road.

"Here he comes." I touched Dad's arm.

"Yeah, here he comes," Dad said. "He's shut off his lights now. Good." It would be harder for Tyeson to see us if he was driving without headlights.

Moonlight gleamed on the silver Bronco as it rolled quietly into the meadow and stopped nearby at the edge of the trees.

Dad nudged me, and the three of us moved slowly back until we stood behind some willow bushes near the water. I don't think I really believed it would be Tyeson until I saw him silhouetted against the Bronco. He left his driver's door open, reached in the back seat and pulled out a gas can.

"Okay. He is really going to do it," Dad whispered in my ear. His hand gripped my arm. "I'm going to get his keys."

"I'll get them." I breathed the words and started to move.

"I'll get them," Trevor said.

Dad's right hand was like a leg-hold trap. His left was probably working the same hold on Trevor. "Don't move from here! I'll get them."

"*Okay*," I whispered fiercely. Trevor said nothing.

Tyeson was almost at the hay shed when I saw Dad dart into the Bronco and out again. It took him less than a second to get the keys and retreat into the darkness under the trees. If Tyeson had turned, he would have seen Dad.

Tyeson walked slowly now toward the hay shed, stopped and looked around. The night was silent. No owls called. No loons laughed into the darkness. Then he moved forward.

Dad slipped back through the trees behind the Bronco until he stood beside us, screened from Tyeson by the fir tree and the scrub willow along the shore.

Moonlight washed the meadow in a pale light bright enough to see Tyeson jerk the can toward the hay pile and walk like a man watering a flower bed around one side of the shed, then back across the path he had already taken and down the other side. Dad was beside me, cursing steadily under his breath, his tension increasing my own. I followed him like a shadow as he moved toward the pump. He knelt down and wrapped the starter cord around his hand. Tyeson set the can down. Dad yanked the cord. The starter whirled, then stopped.

We saw the flare of a cigarette lighter. "Don't!" Dad yelled at Tyeson, but a split second late.

The light arced as Tyeson threw it and the small flame

caught on some hay.

Then everything happened at once as the flame ignited the gas. Fire roared around the base of the shed and shot toward the roof until in seconds there was a wall of flame on three sides. Dad grabbed a fire extinguisher and ran, Trevor after him.

I stood immobilized for a few moments, amazed at the sudden ferocity of the fire. The police must have been surprised as well, for they missed Tyeson. I saw him run for his truck. He jumped in and then immediately jumped out.

The flames crackled as the hay and the wood of the beams ignited. The aluminum roof shuddered and boomed as the sudden heat hit it. I couldn't see Tyeson. Where was he? He had been at his truck, not ten feet from me. Where had he gone?

"Trevor, use this one. I'll get the pump going," Dad shouted across the roar of the flames.

"Karen!" he yelled, "Come on! I need you."

"I'm coming," I yelled back. I ran away from the pump to the fir tree, picked up the second fire extinguisher and pulled the red restraining pin from the handle. One small fire extinguisher seemed a ridiculous weapon against those towering flames, but I was going to use it. I turned as I lifted the extinguisher and ran toward the fire, stopping suddenly as I hit a solid body. I staggered a little, trying to find my balance. "Sorry," I said automatically, and looked up expecting to see one of the RCMP constables.

It was Tyeson.

"You!" He reacted faster than I did, grabbing my hair and yanking me back against him.

I gasped with pain and surprise. Before I could scream, I felt the point of a knife at my throat. I froze.

"Shut up! Just shut up!" Tyeson's voice was a hoarse whisper in my ear. "You try one karate move and I'll drive this knife in." I imagined the knife at my throat, a long, thin blade from the point at my neck to his hand.

"I understand," I croaked. I could hear my instructor's voice in my head. Karate is useless against a weapon. I was not going to be stupidly heroic.

"Move. To your dad's truck." He jerked my arm and shoved me away from the meadow.

"Move, move!"

I felt the knife jab into my back, a sudden sting below my shoulder blade. I stumbled toward the truck. He wasn't just threatening me; he was stabbing me!

For a few seconds fear ruled my body and I lurched along, Tyeson's hand gripping my arm as I tried to keep away from that knife. This was not supposed to be happening. He was supposed to drop the gas can and cry. I took the trail to the truck, but as I hurried awkwardly, half in front of him, half beside him, I started to think. Come on, Karen. You've got to use reason and emotion. Get control. Talk. Make this more normal.

"Look, Mr. Tyeson. Dad has the key to his truck. I can't start it. My own truck is at the house. We can cut through the woods and I can give you the key to it. I keep a spare one hidden in the engine."

He grabbed my hair again, and the sudden pain made me stumble. He yanked me to my knees and held the knife to my throat. This was it! He was crazy enough to kill me. I couldn't raise my arms to chop at him without getting stabbed, and my feet were underneath me and no help at all. Remember *all* your karate, Karen. Breathe. Centre yourself. Get control. I breathed deeply.

"Karen!" I heard my dad bellowing from the meadow. Breathe, Karen. Concentrate on control.

"How many police are there?" Tyeson pulled my hair with a quick, vicious jerk.

"Four," I answered honestly because I couldn't think of anything else.

"Too many. I can't fight all of them. I don't want them to see me. No witnesses. That's the ticket. No witnesses. As long as no one sees me, clearly sees me, they won't be able to swear I was here. I have to get away." His words came in a rush as if they were tumbling through his head in accelerated motion.

It didn't sound promising to me. I was looking at him; I could identify him, therefore he wasn't planning on leaving me alive to do that. This is trouble, Karen. Believe it. He wants you out of his way.

He yanked my hair again. With that pain the fear subsided and I felt the beginnings of anger. It was one thing to be threatened with death, and it was another to be treated like a rag doll. Go with the emotion, I told myself. Trust it. Anger is going to help you.

"You're hurting me, Mr. Tyeson," I said quietly.

He ignored that. "Where is your truck?"

"At the house."

"How far?"

"Half a mile."

"On your feet. You're taking me there and fast."

"Okay." I stood and looked around.

"Move!" He leaned closer. I smelled sweat and a peculiar smell. Was it fear? His breath was warm on my neck. I felt the prick of the knife under my ear. I tried to keep my voice steady.

"I have to figure out where we are first."

"Hurry up!"

I knew exactly where we were, but I was more controlled now, and thinking. We were south of the mill site, north of the lake and west of the old quarry. Kevin, Paula and Mike and I used to play space invaders in these woods. I knew the trails so well I could run them blindfolded. I turned onto the left-hand trail. It went to the quarry and then east to the house. Somewhere inside me a fierce rage began. He was *not* going to kill me.

My mind was working so fast that smoke should have been coming from my ears. Tyeson planned to kill me as soon as we reached my truck, or as soon as he started it, or maybe before that. The knife at my throat was sharp. Tyeson was afraid and so intent on escaping and saving himself that he might cut my throat before he thought about any consequences.

I started talking. "The police will identify your truck."

He grunted. "I'll claim it was stolen."

He might get away with it. The court would at least listen to him.

"The others saw you at the fire, Mr. Tyeson."

"Too dark for a positive identification." He was quiet for a moment and then asked, "Are you all right?"

I couldn't believe he was asking me that.

"I didn't hurt you, did I?"

"I'm all right," I lied.

"I didn't mean to hurt you. I just had to get away. You can see that I had to get away."

"Oh, yes," I said. "Of course. "

"I couldn't be caught there. It would ruin everything. All my plans. Everything."

He sounded so reasonable.

"This is all your father's fault, you know. If he had sold, I wouldn't have had to do any of this. He was in my way. Deadlines were close." His voice was hoarse, intense, as if he were speaking from somewhere deep inside himself. "Two weeks to flip this land or the company will foreclose. Not a bank foreclosure — civilized, tidy and legal. Nothing decent. It's my life they want to foreclose."

Fraser was right. Tyeson was in deep trouble. Whoever was closing down on him was not on my side of the law.

"It will work. Yes." He was muttering to himself now. "The fire. Stewartson will sell. The deal will work. It's my company that's buying it, not me. I can leave and the deal will still go through. The false accounts. I'll get some money from there. I'll wait for the rest. I'll get away."

Even if the hay was gone, even if *I* was gone, I knew that Dad would never sell. He'd borrow from neighbours; he'd cash in his retirement savings; he'd sell the cattle and start over, but he'd never sell the land.

A sudden pain and heavy weight on my shoulder forced me down on the ground. While I'd been thinking, Tyeson had panicked.

"We're lost," Tyeson hissed in my face. His eyes narrowed. "We haven't got time to be lost. You are leading me in circles."

"No, Mr. Tyeson, I know where we are." I should have paid more attention to him and his moods and fears. He could kill me while I was busy thinking about him. The emotions that drove him weren't the quick bright ones or the deep sweet ones that drove me or Kevin; his were dark and confused. They didn't spread warmly to others, but circled inside him, driving him to please only himself. It was a crazy moment to realize that I *did* understand a lot about feelings.

"You're lying. I can't see any lights." He wound his hand in my hair and pulled tighter.

"We have to go around the beaver pond, but we're okay, Mr. Tyeson." I concentrated on blocking out the pain. "I know where we are. It's okay. I'll get us out." I could do polite and respectful really well when I had to.

"I don't want to hurt you, you know that. You're a very pretty girl." He stared at me for a moment. I understood right then how blood feels when it chills in your body. "Too bad. I never wanted to hurt you." He increased the pull on my hair as he spoke.

I watched the knife out of the corner of my eye. He might stab me now.

"Come on. Move." He shook my arm. "Show me the path."

I breathed deeply, trying to get my brain working again. "It's not far," I said as quietly and as calmly as I could. Anger I needed, but not panic.

"Get going."

I knew I was going to die if I didn't do something soon. He wouldn't take long to decide that it would be smarter to kill me now and escape on his own. Only his fear of being lost kept me alive. The minute he knew where he was, the minute he could see the lights of the ranch house, he'd knife me. I'm not sure he knew he was going to do that, but I knew it. He was like a wild man now, panicked by what he'd done, terrified of being caught, but still calculating, still thinking.

We had about five minutes before we would round the curve and he would see the lights. I studied the trail, the way it twisted, which trees stood on the sides, where it dipped and narrowed.

I brought up pictures from the past when Kevin had chased me down this trail and Paula had hidden in the trees. Kevin, Mike and I had cleared a path to trap Paula, but it was so dangerous that we had ended up showing her how it would have worked if we had used it. The trail stopped at the edge of the quarry. A ledge, about a foot and a half wide and eight feet down, ran partway along the cliff face. A fir branch hung over the cliff, and we had practised swinging ourselves down onto that ledge.

The trail was still clear; I just had to remember exactly where I was. My eyes darted back and forth, picking out the trees and shrubs from the shadows in the moonlight. I concentrated on the picture in my mind held there from years ago. Don't think, Karen, just look at the picture. Go into your mind and block out everything else.

As we hurried along, I fitted the trail in front of me, black and white, shadows and moonlight, over the coloured picture in my head until they matched like a photo and a negative. We passed the big fir and then the small birch. Stop thinking, Karen, just go with the picture. Trust your mind. Believe in yourself. Let the anger drive you. We rounded a corner and the lights of the ranch yard twinkled through the trees.

"I see the lights," Tyeson puffed behind me, very close. "Stop here. Stop!"

I relaxed suddenly against him as if I were going to faint. When he loosened his hold and turned toward me, I straightened and chopped up with the edge of my hand. The sudden, violent crack of my hand on his arm broke his grip. I sprinted away. He yelled and started after me, his feet thudding on the soft ground. I ran toward the quarry, he and his knife only inches behind me. Concentrate on the trail, Karen. Two more steps. This was it! I leapt off the trail, grabbed the branch, twisted in the air and dropped over the edge of the quarry. My feet hit the ledge with a jarring thump. I leaned into the cliff wall, hugging it for safety and protection.

I heard a startled cry, shrubs breaking as Tyeson crashed through them, then his shriek as he dropped into space. His hand brushed mine as he clawed for some kind of hold.

He screamed all the way to the bottom, a wild, high scream that floated in the air. I heard the thud as he hit the rocks below.

I held myself perfectly still for a few moments, my mind blank. I couldn't move quickly without risking a fall. I was frozen against the rock wall, one hand gripping a tree root and the fingers of the other pressed into a crack in the rock face. You can't stay here, Karen, I told myself. You could fall. So move. Inch along the ledge. Get back into the picture in your mind. Concentrate. Freeze your feelings now. Don't let them flood through you. Now is no time to feel anything. Ignore Tyeson.

I saw the ledge in my mind as it had been when Kevin

and I were kids. There was a handhold in front of me. It changed from the red root in my mind to a black rope in the pale light. I wrapped my fingers around it, then tried a foothold on another root. It was too small for my foot, but gave me a secure toehold. Just reach for the next root. I shoved myself up another few feet, scraping along the rock. I grabbed a root at the top, pulled myself over, rolled away from the quarry edge and sat leaning my back against a tree.

My hands shook; then my whole body jerked. Fear washed over me.

When the spasm stopped, I felt calm and alive, as if all the nerves on my skin were more sensitive than they had ever been. The breeze seemed cool on my face, my tears salty at the edge of my mouth. I took a deep breath. I was all right. I thought of Kevin. I'm fine, Kevin. I willed the words to him. Words didn't travel very well between us, but emotions did. I thought about the woods and the quiet here. I tried to feel calm, and safe.

Chapter 14

The euphoria of realizing that I was still alive didn't last long. I had time to lose it on my walk back to the lake. My feet began to feel heavy, my legs shaky. My mind, which had been so clear and bright and had moved faster than light earlier, was cloudy and stupid now. The trail back to the meadow seemed miles long.

When I finally stepped through the trees, the fire was dead. All four constables, looking like erratic dancers in the moonlight, were stamping on sparks and trying to extinguish the last of the embers. Trevor was pulling hay from the pile with a pitchfork and flinging it on the ground. I couldn't see Dad.

Will Fraser left the others and hurried toward me, his face streaked with soot, his brown uniform spotted with black burn holes. "Where have you been?" he demanded.

"Where's Dad?"

"He's in the woods looking for you. Where did you go? I told you to stay put. I lost track of you. I lost track of Tyeson." He ranted on. "I had a fire on my hands, Tyeson on the loose, and you missing. Then, when I needed him, Dan tore off to look for you. This is crazy. Everyone off doing their own thing. Civilians! Hah! What kind of operation is this? How am I supposed to report it?"

I stood there while his worry and concern washed over me and felt the terror of the night grow inside. I gulped. "Where's Dad?"

"He's looking for you. What happened?"

"Tyeson put a knife to my throat and forced me into

the woods."

"That didn't happen. Tell me I didn't let that happen."

I felt my jaw tighten. "Yes, it did."

"Oh my God. What a mess! Are you all right? Where's Tyeson?"

"He fell over a cliff and I think he's dead."

Fraser came closer and patted my shoulder. "Take it easy, Karen. It's been a crazy night. Now take a deep breath and tell me where Tyeson is."

I had an insane urge to laugh. Fraser didn't believe me.

"Tyeson fell into the quarry," I said slowly. "It's a long way down and there are rocks at the bottom."

Fraser stepped back. "That's the truth?"

I heard Dad running into the meadow from the quarry trail.

"Fraser, get yourself down this trail. Tyeson's lying at the bottom dead as a log and I CAN'T FIND MY DAUGHTER! We're going to need the dogs."

"Dad."

"If Karen's harmed in any way I'll have your job. Four cops and you couldn't keep your eyes on one man!"

"Dad."

"She was standing back beside the tree. She should have been safe ... Karen?"

"I'm okay, Dad."

"Karen?" He stopped suddenly, then flew at me, grabbed me and hugged me so hard I thought he was going to break my ribs.

"Dad. Hey! Let me go."

He ran his hands over my head and arms, picked me up and hugged me again. Warmth and comfort swirled around me. Then he pushed me away and stared. "So? How did you manage to get Tyeson to jump over a cliff?"

"Dad!" I laughed a little, and he hugged me again.

He kept his arm around my shoulders as I told him,

briefly. "Tyeson was going to knife me. I broke away and jumped over the cliff; he followed; he didn't know the quarry was there."

Fraser had been listening. "You jumped over first?"

"I jumped down to the ledge. I knew it was there; he didn't."

One of the constables called to Fraser. The radio crackled in the squad car.

"I'll need to hear everything later," Will said.

"Sure." Dad squeezed my shoulders and released me.

"The water pump works," I said to Dad.

"Yeah. It caught on the second try. It must have had dirt on the sparkplug."

"How did that happen?"

"I can only guess."

I hadn't been gone twenty minutes, but in that time the tower of flames had been controlled, doused and reduced to ashes. Smoke still drifted from one side of the hay shed. Trevor pitched hay that was smouldering toward a constable who sprayed water on it. It looked as though only the front four feet of the hay pile had been destroyed. The water would ruin more of it, but most of the winter hay looked safe.

The meadow smelled of the spicy incense of burned hay instead of fresh clover and sweet grass. It had changed in other ways too in that short time: it was busy when it had been still; noisy when it had been silent.

One of the cruisers was now parked in the meadow, and a constable yelled into the radio phone to the central office, complaining that he didn't have enough person power. Fraser walked over and told the constable to cancel the order for staff and dogs. He then motioned to me. I walked to the side of the squad car.

"Okay, Karen. Can we go on from here in some kind of order? Where is Tyeson's body?"

"Not far. In the quarry."

"Can we get in with an ambulance?"

I remembered the thud when Tyeson hit the bottom of the quarry. "You can get in with a four-wheel drive. You won't need an ambulance. He's dead."

Fraser nodded, accepting the fact that I was sure. "Okay, but standard procedure says I send in a medic to check." He turned to Dad. "I've called for the Ident. Officer. We'll need pictures and evidence from the scene. Would you guide him to the spot?"

"Sure," Dad nodded. "I'll take Karen home first."

"I'm going to need a statement from you, Karen," Fraser said.

"When?"

"Later. I have to deal with the Ident. Officer and the body recovery first."

"So, Will," Dad said. "Why don't you come to the house for it later?"

I turned away and started toward Dad's truck. I was suddenly very tired. I heard Dad speak to Fraser.

"We'll put the coffee on, then I'll come back and show your Ident. man where the body is. I'll help you bag Tyeson and get him out. After that, we can all go to the ranch house for coffee and something to eat."

Fraser nodded, and we left him trying to instill some order and method into what was left of the night.

When I walked into the house, Mrs. Jennings hugged me. She's not a touchy-feely person, so I was surprised and grateful. I needed hugs tonight.

The Jennings and I sat at the kitchen table, eating the last of Mom's chocolate chip cookies from the freezer while I retold the events of the night. Sarah was in bed, so I didn't have to adjust the story; I just told it the way it had happened. It felt wonderful to be inside the ranch house, in our own kitchen, peaceful and safe. When I finished talking, no one said anything. I stared out the window, not seeing the lake, not even seeing the reflection of the kitchen furniture, but seeing in my mind Tyeson, his anger and his greed.

He was dead, without life, cold. No tomorrows for him. He fell over the cliff onto the rocks and that was that. He died trying to make himself rich. He hadn't been trying to achieve anything wonderful, or prevent anything horrible; he had just wanted to be rich. I didn't understand him and he had never really understood us.

If he had known Dad better, he would have known that Dad wouldn't sell his land because he needed money, and if he had known me better, he would have known I wouldn't just do as I was told. I suppose when he narrowed his world down to money, he couldn't see anything else, and wouldn't have understood anything else. It was all so dumb.

About two hours later, Dad, Trevor and Fraser returned to the house. Fraser had been into town and left Dad and Trevor with the identification crew.

"Are you okay?" Will asked me.

"Skinned knuckles," I said.

"You were lucky."

If *he* had managed to escape Tyeson, he would have said he was trained and efficient. When I did it, I was "lucky." I lifted my head and looked at him. "I knew about the ledge."

"You mean you deliberately jumped over that cliff?"

I nodded.

He looked at Dad. "She was lucky."

"No," Dad said as he poured Will some coffee. "She was smart, levelheaded and courageous." He lifted his cup to me.

"And angry," I said.

Dad nodded.

"But Tyeson died." This was the part I hadn't wanted to

think about. If I hadn't led Tyeson over the cliff, he would not have died.

"Better him than you," Dad said.

I was quiet then.

Fraser opened a briefcase and took out some papers. "I got some information from Tyeson's home office. I haven't read through it, but I think he was supporting a gambling habit. We'll look for evidence in the next few weeks at the bank, at his home and in the books of his related companies. Might find something."

"What did you get on the Shandon Development Company?" I asked.

Fraser shook his head. "I haven't seen anything."

"What about Mrs. Tyeson?" Dad asked. "Did she know anything?"

Fraser looked at the papers for a second, his hands motionless. "That was tough. I had to tell her he was dead and take all his papers. She kept saying they were going to start fresh. They had tickets to some island in the Caribbean and were moving next month. She was . . . distressed. I couldn't tell how much she knew. Probably not much. I got a doctor in to give her some sedation."

I thought about Lydia Tyeson. She had lost her son years ago, and now her husband. Maybe she'd fought with him, but they were a couple, and now she had no one. It would be terrible to be so alone.

I looked at Trevor sitting there, and at Dad, and wondered why they were moving back and forth the way they were.

"Put your head down, Karen," I heard Mrs. Jennings say.

I dropped my head between my knees. I felt Dad's hand at the back of my neck. "Are you okay?"

I couldn't speak as I waited for the room to settle back into place and the ringing in my ears to recede. When the room stopped moving, I raised my head cautiously.

"Here." Dad put a small glass of liquid into my hand. I

sipped it; it tasted bitter.

"Scotch," Dad said. "Sit beside me." He pulled my chair close and put his arm around me. The scotch settled in my stomach like a warm ball of fire and slowly spread into my chest and then into my limbs. I felt warm and, after a few minutes, relaxed.

"Just stay put, Karen," Mrs. Jennings said. I nodded. I let everyone talk without taking part in the conversation or even listening to it for about an hour. Then I started to feel more normal.

"Okay?" Dad asked finally.

"Yeah." I stood, stretched and got myself a cup of coffee. "I'm okay now."

When Trevor rose to leave, I was near the back door, getting more sugar. He stopped.

"I'm sorry, Karen."

I looked at him, surprised. His eyes were wide, and for the first time, I could see sincerity and compassion there. He was probably still impulsive and self-centred, but perhaps more likeable than I had thought. I couldn't hate him. I didn't have any room for hate. I'd seen enough negative emotion from Tyeson tonight to last my lifetime. I suddenly didn't want any of it inside myself. "It's over, Trevor."

"Yeah." He hesitated for a moment, then leaned over and kissed me on the cheek. "Take care of yourself."

I drew back, astounded. "Why, Trevor," I said, staring straight at him. "Does this mean that we might actually be *friends*?"

He grinned. "It's a strange night," he said. "Anything's possible."

I laughed. "Good night and . . . uh, good luck." He had charges and court appearances ahead of him.

"Thanks."

The Jennings went home to their ranch. Fraser left about five-thirty in the morning, after having taken my statement and asking me a thousand questions.

Kevin arrived at six. I had just gotten ready for bed when I saw the lights of his truck in the yard. I knew it was Kevin before I saw the truck. I threw on my robe and met him at the back door.

"You're all right." He grabbed me and hugged me.

"You knew I was, didn't you?"

"Not really. I wasn't sure what was going on. I felt something weird had happened, something scary. Then I felt peace and then terror, and I almost went crazy. I was thirty miles away in the bush. It took me hours to get out."

He held me close, one hand cupping my chin, then trailing along my jaw and sliding into my hair, carefully, as if I were precious or fragile.

"Did you leave your dad and Bob out in the bush without a vehicle?" I tried to stay rational, methodical, dealing with ideas one at a time. We were going to talk, but I was going to be calm.

"No, my dad's truck is there, but they want me back sometime today to haul wood."

I took Kevin into the living room. We sat on the sofa, our shoulders touching, our hands clasped, facing the view of the lake while I told him about my night.

Kevin listened to me, stroking the back of my hand lightly. He tensed and swore when I told him about Tyeson pulling my hair, and ran his hand through it gently as if trying to erase the hurt. Soothing. Comfortable.

I started to tremble when I told him about Tyeson plunging over the cliff's edge. He held me close. The problem that had been simmering in my mind broke through then, and I let the worry and fear take shape.

"I couldn't think of anything else to do, Kev. But what if I was wrong?" I cried then, big tears and heaving sobs. I

felt like a blithering, sniffing, sodden mess of worry and
anxiety. So much for staying calm. Kevin stroked my hair
and let me cry. Finally I dragged out all the tissues in my
pocket, wiped my eyes and blew my nose. "What if he
wasn't going to kill me? I led him to his death. I'll never
know if that was the right thing to do."

He spoke quietly. "Maybe you'll never know for sure
whether he was going to kill you, but letting him fall
seemed to be your only choice at the time, didn't it?"

I nodded. "He said that he didn't want to hurt me, but
he did. So I thought that as much as he didn't want to kill
me, he would. Was I wrong?"

"I don't know, Kay. But you had to make some kind of
decision, and you have to live with it."

I sat back. "I think he would have killed me. I guess
that makes it easier." Then my voice wobbled a little. "But
I'm not sure."

He rocked me in his arms as if I were a child. We sat
like that for a long time. The morning air was pale and
still, the lake calm. Mist rose in wispy tendrils near the
shore. A loon paddled far out on the lake, silent in this
early hour.

"It's all right," I said finally. "I'm all right." I leaned
back against his hand and looked at him, catching the
edge of fear in his eyes before humour softened them.

"I wish I'd been here when it happened."

I studied him then in the soft light. He was so honest
about how much he cared for me. I needed to be honest
as well.

"I do love you, Kevin."

He started to hug me, then hesitated. "Why do I hear a
'but' in there?"

I laughed. "You know me so well."

"But?" he said.

"I was thinking."

"Hah! The rational Karen is back."

"I guess so."

"You love me, but?" he prompted.

"But you can't be here all the time. You'll be away. I'll be away. I have to live my own life, make my own decisions and my own mistakes."

"Believe me, honey. You will make your own decisions. It's not possible to take over on you. You are the most independent, focused, ambitious, opinionated woman I know. A man would have to be Superman to even influence you."

"I'm not that strong."

"You seem that way to me."

That surprised me. I didn't know he saw me that way. I saw myself as much weaker, and less wise.

He had heard my concern and spoke slowly. "I'll try to stay out of your decisions, but when you love someone, it's not easy to stand back."

"I know that." It wasn't easy for me to let Sarah make her own decisions.

"But . . . ."

"But what?"

"I'll stay out of your decisions, but I need to know what you feel. Don't shut me out. I want to be there for you."

He was there, like the wind off the lake, like the sun on my skin, like my own heartbeat. "I'm not going to be able to shut you out anymore, Kev. You're part of me now."

Kevin kissed me then, and I kissed him back. Waves of feeling flooded through me, tumultuous, overwhelming and powerful. Bubbles sparkled along my veins; froth scattered my thoughts. I felt his hands on my shoulder and waist, pulling me closer as if those hands were inside me, caressing me, creating the waves, increasing the power of the feelings.

We broke apart. I took a long, ragged breath. Kevin rested his forehead on mine.

"Man, Karen."

"Me too," I said. It was all I could manage. My brain didn't seem to be connected to my tongue.

He took a deep breath. "We'll take it easy, okay? We've got years."

"Years," I nodded. I'd probably agree with anything he said right then.

"Your dad's home."

"Uh-huh."

"Your sister's here."

"Uh-huh." He was right. We weren't alone. Sensible. I had to be sensible. Where was the practical Karen that I relied on? I took another deep breath and pushed myself off the sofa until I was standing. "Good night," I said dreamily.

"Good night." He looked up, raised an eyebrow and grinned at me.

I yawned. He laughed. I was suddenly exhausted. He was right; we had years. I fetched a blanket and pillow from the hall closet and tossed them across the room. "Crash, love. It's a long drive back into the bush. Good night. Good night. Umm . . . good night. The sofa is pretty comfortable."

I heard him chuckle as I closed my bedroom door. He was gone when I woke up.

Chapter 15

When I got out of bed at noon, the message light on the answering machine was blinking furiously. News travels quickly in our community: the husband of the police dispatcher works at the gas station, the wife of the Ident. man was the check-out clerk at the grocery store.

There was a message by the phone from Dad. "Mom coming home today!!!"

That was wonderful. I wanted to talk to her so badly I could almost feel words shaping themselves and lifting off my tongue. Tonight, then, I could give her back her life. She could have her mail route. She could have her cooking and her housecleaning and her laundry and running Sarah to Heather's place and all the other things she did. Tonight I would be an ordinary student again.

"You're finally up. I thought you were going to sleep all day." Sarah ran through the kitchen, picking up an apple from the counter.

"Hold it," I said. She stopped for a second, like a hummingbird poised to dart away. "Where's Dad?"

"In the sheep pen with Montgomery." She wrinkled her nose. "I had to help get Montgomery into the pen. I hate that ram. He tried to butt me again."

"He always does."

"He didn't get me today. I'm way too fast for him."

"Where are you going?"

She ignored me. "Did you hear Mom was coming home today?"

"Yes."

"You won't be able to boss me anymore."

"Get out of here, Sarah."

She moved, but turned at the door. "The day is going to drag. It'll be like having the last period at school for the whole day, just waiting, waiting."

"I know."

The door banged behind her.

I found Dad in the sheep pen. He was bending over Montgomery, cleaning the ram's feet and dabbing on medication.

He raised his head. "Everything okay?"

"Yeah. Sarah's around here somewhere. I'm not sure where."

"She won't go far today."

I watched him carve Montgomery's hoof and pick the dirt out of the ram's foot. He worked meticulously, steadily and did a thorough job. Montgomery bucked once. Dad held him tight against his legs until the ram was again quiet and still.

"So Mom's coming home today."

He looked up. "She called this morning when you were sleeping."

"What did she say?"

"That she's coming home and, to tell you the truth, Karen, after she said that I didn't hear anything else except the time the plane gets in." Dad straightened, put Montgomery's feet back onto the floor, made sure the ram was secure on his feet, then opened the pen door. "Four o'clock."

I leapt for the fence as Montgomery headed straight for me, and watched as he nailed the fence below my feet with a thud. "That's great, Dad."

"Yeah," he said. "Wonderful."

"Missed her, did you?" I looked over his head as I looked at the house beyond the sheep pens, at the dogs chasing each other around the tractor, at the lake shimmering in the hot sunshine. I caught a glimpse of Sarah's red T-shirt at the lakeshore. She was probably fishing. A frog boomed a complaint somewhere near her. Mom must have missed us and all this with a fierce pain. I looked back at Dad as he turned to me. I could see the tears in his eyes.

"Yes, I missed her. Never doubt that. Like the breath in my body, I missed her. The pipes are going to dance tonight, Karen. The balloons are going up and we are going to have a party." He let out a whoop of joy so loud that Montgomery panicked and ran out the gate and into the pasture. We watched him go, Dad's excited yell still ringing in the air.